Parables of Lucas Fosterman

Jason Mayer

This work, including all characters, names, and places:
Copyright 2017 Jason Mayer, unless otherwise noted.
Cover layout by Rayvision Design, Inc.
Cover art by Aletia and Evgeny Atamanenko from Bigstock.com.
Interior layout by Edward Gehlert.
Interior art by Dvarg and Makc from Bigstock.com.
Beta Reading by Jamie Mattingly and Abrahm Beezley.
Editing services provided by Edward Gehlert.

Happy Duck Publishing
PO Box 607
Belle, MO 65013

Genre: Fiction, General
ISBN: 978-0-9861182-3-4
First Edition.

This book is dedicated to my fourth-grade teacher Mrs. Koenig, who first lit my passion to write, and to my wife Angela who is more committed to shaping young minds than anyone I know. God bless all teachers!

Acknowledgements

I would like to thank my great friend Edward Gehlert for all his encouragement and guidance over the years. He has always seen me as greater than I truly am, which has helped drive me to be a better person. I would also like to thank his lovely wife Eva, for supporting Ed in his goal to help others live out their dreams. You both deserve the best that the future has to offer.

Thank you to all the Combat Correspondents and other Marines with whom I served. The eight years I spent in the Marine Corps taught me a lot about being a writer, man, husband and eventually a father.

My business partners Charles and Bob have been great friends and mentors through the years. Thank you for helping me feed my family and keep the lights on.

Whether I needed graphic design help or a spare room to stay in, Ray, you have always been there for me whenever I needed a friend.

Jamie and Abe were very helpful in reading through the first drafts of these stories and giving me their guidance and opinions on how to make the book more cohesive.

I would also like to acknowledge all the family, friends, and business associates who have been with me on this journey.

Finally, I would like to thank my boys Noah and Caleb for encouraging me to make up stories at night. You have shown me that the world still craves new stories, no matter how corny or horribly told they may be at times. I hope you both continue to enjoy writing and telling stories of your own.

Contents

Prologue

"Man is the cruelest animal."

– Fredrick Nietzsche

The Bitter Darkness

Ten-year-old Katie moaned as she started to wake. She felt dizzy and her mouth was dry. Her long blonde hair was matted to her face and neck, held in place by a mix of sweat and dirt. She sat up slowly, holding her heavy head in her small hands. She rubbed her eyes trying to focus in the darkness.

As her eyes began to clear, she could see a thin sliver of light coming through a crack on the other side of the room. The light was just bright enough for her to see that she was in a barn. She looked down to see that she was sitting in a pile of hay. She scratched at her legs, which had become itchy and red. She smoothed the sides of her white dress down around her ankles to shield her legs from the sharp sprigs of hay.

She was terrified. Nothing made sense. Where was she? How did she get here? How long had she been asleep? Where was her mom, her dad, anyone?

Something deep inside told her not to cry. Even without any answers, she knew she had to stay strong.

She tried to clear her mind and review her last memories. She could remember riding her pink bike around the neighborhood.

She could remember riding to Wanda's house and playing basketball. She could remember leaving Wanda's house and heading for home. Then nothing…

She was having a hard time keeping her head clear and could not shake the dizziness. Her chest was very tight. She tried to take in a deep breath. She wheezed loudly as she worked to fill her lungs. She had always been asthmatic, and the hay was making it almost impossible for her to breathe. She could tell that her lips were tight and knew that they were likely deep blue from lack of oxygen.

She broke into a coughing fit, covering her mouth with her hands out of instinct. That's when she smelled it. A strong odor on her hands. It reminded her of her mom's nail polish remover, only sweeter. The unique smell forced an image to flash through her mind. It was the image of a large man with a scruffy beard and blue shirt.

Slowly, her memories started to fill back in. The man had dropped a box full of Girl Scout cookies and was picking them up. She had stopped to help him when the man grabbed her and put a rag over her face. She remembered smelling the strong odor, then feeling dizzy and sleepy.

This time she couldn't hold back the tears. She began sobbing, softly at first, then harder as she could see the dim crack of light begin to widen. The barn door creaked open. The tears began streaming down her cheeks as the man in the blue shirt appeared in the doorway and started walking toward her.

She opened her mouth to scream, but no sound came out. The horror was so overwhelming that she didn't even notice that her breathing had completely stopped.

Katie stared at the man with wide, watery eyes. She could feel the dizziness and blackness pressing down on her. She didn't fight it. Instead, she allowed it to overtake her mind and body.

Even as the man's shadow engulfed her small frame, it was too late. Katie had already fallen back into the bitter darkness.

Paving the Path to Forgiveness

"The weak can never forgive. Forgiveness is the attribute of the strong."

— *Mahatma Gandhi*

Spring 2006

A Mostly Peaceful Drive

Lucas Fosterman enjoyed the wind blowing through his gray hair as he sped along the Pacific Coast Highway in a beautiful blue Shelby GT 500 convertible. The new model sports car wasn't as cool as the 1965 Shelby he had driven once as a younger man, but it still made him feel like the king of the road.

His biggest regret was that his late wife Sarah wasn't by his side yelling at him to slow down while squeezing his arm with excitement. He had thought about her a lot during his three-week vacation.

He had started in the Seattle area roaming the streets of the city and eating at the best restaurants in town. Then he spent a few days in the San Juan Islands touring the small towns and riding ferries from island to island.

After Seattle, he had driven down the coast through Portland, Napa Valley, San Francisco and Monterey. He had avoided the interstate as much as possible and stuck to the coastal roads enjoying the sights, sounds, and smells of the ocean.

He was now entering the last leg of his journey. He had strategically waited until late afternoon before entering Los Angeles to avoid the traffic. His plan had worked for a while, but eventually the LA traffic engulfed him. The thrill of driving a convertible sports car quickly faded as the smell of smog from thousands of exhaust pipes filled his nostrils. Plus, his old legs began to ache from working the break and clutch on the manual transmission.

After nearly two hours of aggravation, the traffic finally released him to begin speeding through Orange County and down towards San Diego. It was now fully dark, and he could see the skyline of the city shining like a beacon. As he entered the downtown area, he became nostalgic at the sight of the large gray Navy ships in the distance. His excitement grew as he turned onto Harbor Drive and saw the hulking mass of his old friend, the *USS Midway*. Tomorrow he planned to spend the whole day touring the decks of his former duty station before flying back home to Missouri.

But for tonight he just headed across the Coronado Bridge toward the Hotel del Coronado. He left his car with the valet and checked in.

Three Drinks

Lucas wasted no time settling into his room. He left his suitcase mostly packed and just pulled out a dress shirt, pair of slacks, and grooming bag. He took a long hot shower to soothe his sore muscles, but he still felt a little tense from sitting in the cramped car all day.

He moaned out a few stretches as he got dressed and headed down the elevator to the lobby.

Sitting down at the posh hotel bar, Lucas ordered an Old Fashioned. The choice was a bit highbrow for his usual tastes, but he knew this location was famous for its classic cocktails. Instead of using cherry and orange juice, they muddled whole cherries and orange wedges into a paste. They also used homemade bitters and the finest rye whiskey. Lucas preferred bourbon in most every case, but for an Old Fashioned he felt bourbon was a tad too sweet when combined with the other ingredients in the beverage.

He took a hearty swallow and sat back in his chair letting the stress from a long day on the road melt away. He felt much better now that he was settled into the quiet bar with a good stiff drink.

Lucas had tried to limit himself to a two-drink maximum for most of his adult life. A number of bad decisions as a young man and a family tree plagued with alcoholics made it clear that he needed to place a firm governor on his drinking. This act of self-limitation became even more important once he became a father and later a grandfather.

He was a bit surprised at how easy the first drink went down. He ordered a second one, and watched silently as the bartender went through the three-minute process of "creating" the cocktail, as she termed it.

He chatted with the pretty redhead for a few minutes until he discovered that he had already emptied his second glass. He felt a twinge of guilt, but ordered a third drink. He was a grown man on vacation after all.

After delivering the third cocktail, the bartender moved down to the other side of the bar to take the orders of three businessmen who had just arrived.

Lucas was left alone with his thoughts. As he pulled the short tumbler up to his lips he caught a glimpse of himself in the bar's antique mirror. He was a little disappointed with what he saw.

His silver hair showed every bit of his sixty-six years. The dark circles under his eyes and deep lines on his forehead gave away the sadness that had invaded his life over the past decade. He was still in decent shape for a "senior citizen." His tall and slim frame held up strong shoulders and toned arms from years of woodworking and carving. But most of his positive features had withered with age. He sagged in places, wrinkled in others, and wasn't at all impressed with his posture.

He sat down his drink and ran his fingers through his unkempt hair feeling a bit self-conscious. He looked around the bar and saw that it was mostly empty. The only other people around were the bartender and three businessmen.

What was his problem? No one had any interest in an old man sitting alone at a bar. He laughed at himself and went back to finishing his drink.

The Quietness of Night

As Lucas brushed his teeth in preparation for bed, he felt a small wave of depression wash over him. Bedtime had become a hard and melancholy time for him over the past year. During the day he could distract himself with television, short walks, peaceful drives, and other activities. But at night he was left with nothing but quiet darkness and lonely thoughts.

After Sarah died it was hard for Lucas to quiet his mind at night. He would lie awake wondering what she was doing up there. Could she see him, or was she too busy running the golden streets of Heaven?

He had no doubt that she was in Heaven. She had always been a good Christian woman and a kind and gentle soul. He just hoped he would see her again... given the actions he planned to take in the next couple of days.

He shook off the thoughts and moved on to more positive things. He went over his itinerary for tomorrow. Get up early. Have a nice breakfast outside by the ocean. Spend the day touring the *USS Midway*. Eat a great seafood dinner. Board the plane. Drive home from the airport. And then...

Again he tried to shake off the thoughts, but this time his memories had nowhere to hide. He concentrated on blanking out his mind and trying to fall asleep. It worked for a while, then he started to see glimpses of long wispy blonde hair and the silhouette of a ten-year-old girl. He could hear laughing and see the silhouette spinning around while playing in an open field. He tried again to block out the images, but it wasn't working. It never worked.

"Katie..." He whispered as tears started to fall. "My precious little Katie."

A Mostly Good Day

The next morning Lucas woke up groggy, but still excited about his day. He got dressed in his Sunday finest, threw on his U.S. Marine Veteran cap and waited for room service to bring him breakfast. He decided to eat on the patio outside his room, which had a nice view of the Pacific Ocean. After breakfast, he took a stroll along the beach thinking about nothing but blue skies while watching the birds scavenge for food.

At around 10 am, he jumped in his rented Shelby and headed back across the Coronado Bridge toward the *USS Midway*. He couldn't believe how excited and nervous he was as he pulled into the parking lot. He hadn't been on the ship for more than forty years, but something inside made him feel like a young man getting ready to embark on another new adventure.

He purchased a ticket and walked up to the gangplank. He looked up at the giant gray hunk of metal and marveled at how majestic the decommissioned ship looked as it sat peacefully tethered to the boardwalk. Even with a few marketing banners strung up on its railings, the old ship still stood proud and unique among all the modern boats and busy tourists that filled the downtown San Diego Harbor.

As he walked up the gangplank he saluted the flag for old-times-sake and entered the main hanger deck. He spent nearly three hours visiting the lower decks of the ship, letting memories wash over him in every section.

He had spent over a year on the vessel in the mid 1960's serving as a sergeant helping to provide security. Tensions were high back then as it was the middle of the Vietnam War. Most of his daily activities involved breaking up fights and guarding one hatch or another as the higher ups discussed secret missions. His longest days were when he had brig duty, but he made the most of his time reading books and writing letters back home to Sarah and others. His favorite times were escorting VIP's, like visiting admirals and USO acts. But that didn't happen very often.

Lucas finally made his way up to the flight deck. It was an impressive display showcasing more than twenty aircraft scattered throughout the massive deck. He was most excited to see a Douglas A-1 Skyraider sitting there in all its glory.

He would never forget the day that pilots from one of Midway's A-1 squadrons scored the first kill from Navy aviators in the war by gunning down a MIG-17 over Southeast Asia. On that day in June 1965, the men on the *USS Midway* felt like they were truly part of a fighting force. He could still hear the cheers from the crewmembers as the triumphant pilots from Strike Fighter Squadron 25 made their way to the Bridge to report to the Air Boss.

After checking out the planes, he made his way to the end of the flight deck and leaned against the railing. From this vantage point he could see the entire San Diego Harbor. He could see everything from yachts to sail boats to cruise ships. The harbor was buzzing with activity. In the distance he could see the *USS Theodore Roosevelt*, "The Big Stick" as he heard one active-duty sailor walking by call it. The massive aircraft carrier looked like a floating island with its immense flight deck and huge arsenal of jet fighters. In 1965 the *Midway* was one of the largest carriers in the fleet, but next to the Roosevelt it might as well have been a frigate.

Before leaving the ship, he decided to take a tour of the brig. The brig was located on the other side of the ship and away from the main tour route. If visitors missed the small sign showing the entrance, they would probably miss the area altogether.

Lucas was amazed at how little had changed from the last time he had seen the small prison. The walls were still painted glossy white and the cell bars were still gray and heavy. Even the smells were the same, a mix of rust and fresh paint. He took a seat in the metal chair where he had stood post for hundreds of hours during his time on board.

He was alone in the small area, so he decided to close his eyes and let his mind drift back in time.

He remembered the letters he wrote to Sarah and how elated he was every time he received a new one from her. He smiled as he remembered pulling into the harbor in Alameda, California, his final port of call. Sarah had flown in from Kentucky to meet him. From the flight deck he could see that she was wearing his favorite bright yellow sun dress. He would never forget that image as she stood there with her long black hair blowing in the breeze, waving wildly at him from the pier. He knew in that moment that he would marry her, and he did six months later. He recalled leaving the Marines and going back home to Missouri to join his uncle's business building custom wood furniture. He thought about he and Sarah moving into their first home together on Cherry Street, the birth of his first son Mark and second son Paul. He remembered how scared he was when he took a risk and started his own woodworking business, eventually opening a showroom in the antique district. He smiled again when he thought about his two boys joining the company and helping to turn it into a successful family business. He thought about the birth of his grandson Tyler, and how proud he was to be a new grandpa. He thought about Katie... His precious little Katie with her beautiful blonde hair...

Just then, the giggle of a small boy startled him. Lucas jumped up from the chair. He quickly turned his head away from the boy to wipe away a little water from his eyes.

"Look Daddy, it's a jail," said the boy who couldn't have been more than seven.

"On a ship, they call it a brig," said the boy's father as he nodded to Lucas.

Lucas nodded back as he walked through the hatch to the main hanger bay. Dazed from the memories, he decided it was time to head back to the hotel. As he crossed over the Coronado Bridge, he took one last look at the old ship.

The rest of the afternoon Lucas walked around in a bit of a haze. The memories had been more overwhelming than he expected. He had one last meal sitting on his patio by the ocean before packing his bags and heading to the airport. He turned in his rental car, shuffled through the security lines, and waited for his plane to board. As he sat in the waiting area he felt his stomach start to knot up. He decided to grab some snack crackers and a bottle of ginger ale to calm his nerves. After eating a few crackers his nerves settled a bit, and he was relieved to hear the gate agent call for the first-class passengers to board.

As he boarded the plane, he was happy to hear that the flight would be less than half full. He took his seat in the first-class cabin and tried not to make eye contact with the other passengers as they walked by. He wasn't use to flying first class, and he felt a bit guilty for some reason. When he set up the trip a few months ago he had decided to splurge a little, knowing it would be the last flight of his life.

The Restless Flight Home

Lucas was happy when the flight attendant closed the doors, and even happier when he realized that no one would be sitting next to him.

He ordered a Jack and Coke from the nice lady and sat back in his chair looking out the window at the Marine Corps Recruit Depot located across from the airport runway. His mind started to drift back to his days at Marine boot camp, but he quickly dismissed the thoughts. He had spent too much time dwelling in the past today.

The first hour of the flight was calm. He read the newspaper, ate a little food, and downed a second Jack and Coke. He decided to close his eyes a bit and take a nap.

With his eyes closed, Lucas couldn't stop his mind from wandering. This time he decided not to stop the images and just embraced his thoughts.

He had gone through a lot in the last several weeks. He had cashed out his entire retirement fund, well over $1.5 million. It had taken quite a bit of work to get the banks to release his money to him all in cash. His financial advisor was convinced that he was senile or possibly suicidal. It was even harder to convert the bulk of that money into gold and silver bars and coins. It's easy to invest in precious metals, but it took quite a bit of work to find companies that would just sell him pure gold and silver without asking a lot of questions. He was sure he had gotten some lousy rates for most of the gold and silver he bought, but it really didn't matter.

Leading up to the trip, he spent months in his workshop building three small lock boxes. He built one out of oak for his son Mark, one out of cherry for his son Paul, and one out of ash for his grandson Tyler. He had worked with all three boys long enough to know exactly what type of wood and stains to use for each box. He spared no expense in picking out the finest hinges and clasps. He even ordered expensive antique locks and found a store that sold imported crushed velour to line the insides. He spent countless hours carving intricate designs into each box using symbols and images he knew would fit the personalities of each boy. He wanted to make sure that each one showcased his years of craftsmanship and experience, as well as his love for the future owners. In the end, he was pleased with the results.

He also spent several weeks planning his trip to the West Coast. He searched through old picture albums and post cards to remind himself of the best restaurants, hotels, and tourist stops. It took him several phone calls to find a rental car company that could accommodate renting him a Shelby GT 500 convertible.

He made a detailed itinerary for the trip, mapped out every stop, made every hotel and restaurant reservation in advance, and even timed out where he would be for every sunset. He wanted the trip to be as perfect as possible. He wanted to re-visit every wonderful location that he and Sarah had visited during their honeymoon and anniversary trips.

The day before flying to Seattle to start his trip he invited his family over for dinner. He ordered food from his favorite restaurant and even picked up an assortment of deserts from the local French bakery. He wanted it to be a wonderful evening.

Paul was there with his wife of five years, Debbie. They didn't have any kids and probably never would given their independent streaks and love of adventure.

Mark was there and brought his ex-wife Lisa. They had been divorced for a few years now, but were still friends. The breakup had been more about Lisa needing some time alone than from any real animosity between the two. Lucas was happy to see that they had arrived together. Mark had expressed some hesitation when Lucas told him he wanted to invite Lisa, but Mark eventually gave in.

Lucas' grandson Tyler was there, along with his new girlfriend Amanda. Lucas' brother Steve and his sister Tammy also drove in for the evening.

They spent the afternoon and evening eating great food, having drinks, and talking about some of their favorite memories together. Toward the end of the night, Lucas decided he needed to make a toast to the ones they had lost along the way. He mentioned his parents and a few family friends. He mentioned his Uncle Frank and older brother Tom. He said a few heart-warming words about his lovely Sarah. And, of course, there was Katie…

At that point Lisa had to leave the table, and the air was sucked out of the room. Mark waited a few seconds before heading out to check on her. Lucas felt horrible, and everyone sat at the table in contemplative silence for several minutes before Paul finally broke the tension by saying it was time for him and Debbie to head out. He had to open the showroom tomorrow morning, so he wanted to get to bed at a decent hour. The others followed Paul's lead, getting up from the table.

Everyone said their goodbyes and hugged Lucas wishing for him to have a great vacation. After everyone left Mark came back inside. He had walked Lisa back to her house, which was just a few blocks away. He then started to pick up a few empty glasses, but Lucas told him to sit down at the kitchen table for a night cap.

They sat in silence for a while just nursing their drinks.

Neither Lucas nor Mark were big talkers, but they had always enjoyed being in each other's presence. Sometimes it was just enough to have someone else in the room that understood your current lot in life.

"Mark, I have something I need to talk to you about," Lucas said breaking the silence. "I just need you to listen... not ask questions and not offer advice. I made up my mind about this a long time ago, and there is nothing you or anyone else can do to stop things from moving forward at this point. You won't understand everything I have to say and that is by design."

Mark sat up in his chair and gave his dad a confused look. "Okay, I guess."

"I am really proud of what you and Paul have been able to do with the business over the past couple of years. Signing over ownership to you guys was one of the highlights of my life. I have always felt guilty cashing the profit sharing checks you guys send me every month, but I understand why you felt it was necessary. However, I am going to ask you to stop sending those checks moving forward."

"I also want you to know that I sold the house to your Uncle Steve a few months ago. He agreed to rent it to me for as long as I need it, so I am still set for housing."

"All my credit cards are paid off and I have no debt. I have cleaned out my retirement account and closed all my accounts."

"I know this all sounds ominous, but I assure you that I am not going to jump off a cliff or anything. You know I believe in the Bible and what it says about suicide. That is not what this is about."

"I am an old man, and I just want to get all my affairs in order. Plus, there is one last thing I must do to make our family whole. These past few years have been very hard on all of us, and I just can't move on until I am sure that all of you can find a path to forgiveness."

"That is all I can tell you for now. We will talk more when I get home from my trip. Now, go home and get some sleep. Take care of Lisa and Tyler, and I will see you in a few weeks.

The Drive Home

The sound of the captain announcing their ascent into St. Louis jolted Lucas from his hazy day-dream. His heart immediately started racing for no apparent reason, but he knew that wasn't going to stop anytime soon. He fidgeted with getting his things together and sat impatiently as the plane moved painfully slow toward the gate. The flight attendant opened the doors and he headed to the exit. She gave him a wink as he left and told him to have a nice evening. For a second he thought that maybe she was on to him, but he quickly realized that was just silly paranoia.

As he reached the top of the gateway and entered the airport, he realized he was rushing. He made a conscious effort to calm himself and slow down. He made his way over to the water fountain and took a few long drinks. He headed into the bathroom, used the urinal, and washed his hands. While throwing away the paper towel he took a quick glance at himself in the mirror. The sight caught him off guard, and he stepped in to take a closer look. He looked pale and clammy. Beads of sweat dotted his forehead. He grabbed another handful of paper towels and dabbed his forehead. He took a few breaths and said aloud, "Calm down... you still have a lot to get done."

Lucas exited the bathroom and found himself moving at a more routine pace. He passed through security and caught the escalator down to the luggage carousel. Thankfully, he didn't have to wait long for the bags to start dropping down from the conveyor belt.

After grabbing his luggage, he caught the shuttle to long-term parking and piled his stuff in the back of his old pickup. He felt more at ease being in familiar surroundings. He had owned the old Chevy pickup for about forty years, and it fit him like a glove.

On the outside it looked like a typical old beater. It still had every small dent, scratch, and spot of faded paint that it had earned over the years. The only clue that it was cared for was a heavy dose of clear coat that gave somewhat of a glossy shine to the blue and white paint. However, under the hood and inside the cab of the truck were as new as anything you could buy off the showroom floor. The vehicle had every modern convenience including a multi-disk CD player, power windows, and an air conditioning that could create ice blocks. The HT 383 engine was less than two years old, along with the transmission and almost every part of the truck that couldn't be seen from the outside.

He turned the key and the truck roared to life. Even for a man in his mid-sixties he still got a kick out of the rumble made by the massive engine.

His nerves continued to calm as he got on the freeway and started the two-hour drive back home. His heart was still racing, but at least he had stopped sweating and could breathe normal again. It was a cool night, so he decided to ride with the windows down to feel the wind on his face. This would be his last road trip in his trusty old Chevy, and he wanted to make the most of it.

He kept himself entertained on the ride home by reliving some of the best moments he had spent in the old truck.

He remembered buying it new in 1966. He told Sarah that he needed it as a work truck, but in reality he just wanted to get rid of his old beat up 55 Ford. Sarah always complained when she had to climb into the truck, especially after he put on some larger tires. But he knew she enjoyed sitting next to him on the long bench seat during road trips.

He recalled driving home from the hospital when Mark was born. There were no car seat laws in those days, and he would never forget the image of Sarah holding the little baby in her arms sitting right next to him.

He remembered dropping Paul off at the airport as he headed off to Marine Corps boot camp. Lucas was so proud when Paul told him he was going to follow in his footsteps and join the Marines. He also remembered feeling relief when he picked Paul back up at that same airport eight years later after being honorably discharged. He had grown into a hulking man by that time, but he still had little Paul's smile and laugh.

He recalled helping Mark move into his first home with his new bride Lisa. They were such a happy young couple.

He remembered driving like a mad man to the hospital when Tyler had fell off his bike, split his head open, and broke his collar bone. Lucas was sure Lisa was going to kill him for letting it happen to her son, but she just hugged Lucas and told him "boys will be boys."

He could remember his precious little Katie… No, he wasn't ready to let his mind go there yet. He just shook away the images and kept his eyes focused on the road ahead. Still, he couldn't completely force away all the memories. Out of the corner of his eye, he could see the faded image of a sweet little girl wearing a white dress and pretty little flower bows in her long blonde hair. Oh Katie, his precious little Katie…

It was almost midnight when he pulled into his garage. He decided not to spend any time unpacking or even getting out of his clothes. Instead he just kicked off his shoes, sat down in his recliner, and pushed it back. His heart was still pounding, but he was exhausted. He just needed to close his eyes for a few minutes.

The Big Day

Lucas was surprised to be woken up by the sun streaming through the living room window. Somehow he had managed to sleep peacefully through the night, something that had not happened in months. He was even more surprised that his heart had stopped racing. He felt calm, relaxed, even peaceful.

He got up, unloaded his bags from the truck, unpacked, and started a load of laundry. The only food left in the house was a pack of powdered donuts and a can of root beer. He watched the morning news as he ate, then started a second load of laundry. He took a shower and got dressed. Nothing fancy, just jeans and a t-shirt.

He spent the rest of the morning doing some light housework, which didn't take long. Before he left for his trip, he had mostly cleaned out the fridge and pantry and made sure everything was left tidy and clean. He folded his laundry and put it all back in the same suitcases he had used for his trip. His closet, drawers, and master bathroom were completely spotless. He went through the house room-by-room and made sure everything was put away. He didn't want to leave a mess for anyone to deal with.

At 11:30 am, he decided it was time to head out. He grabbed his keys and wallet and clipped on the concealed carry holster for his pistol. He walked into his bedroom and stopped at the small safe sitting on his nightstand.

He put his index finger on the biometric lock. The door popped open. Reaching in, he pulled out a custom .45 caliber 1911 pistol.

Lucas had received the pistol as a retirement gift from his boys a few years ago. It was a stainless-steel model with cocobolo grips and beautiful engravings throughout. It was made to be concealed carried, sporting a 4.25 inch commander-style slide and single stack design. The mainspring housing had been bobtailed and all the sharp points had been dehorned. Before receiving the 1911 he would carry on occasion, but after receiving the gift from his sons he felt obligated to carry it whenever feasible.

He pulled out the magazine and checked the chamber. He had cleaned the pistol thoroughly before leaving for his trip, but he wanted to double check anyway. He wiped off a little piece of lint before reinserting the loaded magazine. He racked the slide to chamber a round and engaged the safety before holstering the pistol and pulling his untucked shirt over the grip.

He gave the house one last review before walking over to the calendar tacked on the wall next to the garage door. He looked at the date and double checked the written entry – Doctor Pilter's Office | Friday | 1:30 pm. He really didn't need to double check the time and date. The information had been stuck in his head for almost three months now… ever since fate had intervened and allowed him to see the appointment in the receptionist's log at his doctor's office.

He turned off the lights and jumped in his old truck. He hesitated for a moment as he gripped the key that was stuck in the ignition. He couldn't believe how calm he was. Yesterday he had been a ball of nerves, but now he was steady. He decided not to overthink the situation and turned the key. The engine roared to life and he pulled out of the garage and backed down the long driveway. He spent a couple more moments looking over the house one last time before speeding off toward the downtown area.

As he entered the small town, he smiled as he saw that all the businesses were filled to the brim with customers. He had been a part of the business community for so long that he knew the owners of every shop in town. There was Howard's Hardware, Marconi Shoes, Terry's Flower Shop, and on, and on. He had really loved being a part of this town, and he was going to miss it.

He went through the first of three stop lights in town, which meant that he was entering the antique district. Both sides of the street were filled with a variety of antique shops, art galleries, pottery stores, and other artsy venues. At the end of the block stood Fosterman Custom Furniture, its large carved wood sign hanging from the tall brick façade. He slowed down to a crawl as he passed by his old showroom and looked in the big plate-glass windows. He could see both his boys standing behind the long counter helping customers. He knew they would be there on a Friday summer afternoon. This was peak selling season, and he was happy to see that they were busy.

He drove past the second light and turned right on Broad Street. A few blocks down, he turned into the parking lot. On the left was the Broad Street Diner. To the right was a small medical complex that housed several doctor's offices.

It was only 12:30 pm, so he decided to head over to the diner and grab a bite to eat. He walked in and sat at the counter.

"Hello Lucas." A young waitress greeted him.

"Hello Christy. How are you today."

"I'm fine. Just trying to stay out of the sun. What can I get you today?"

"I'll take a hamburger, fries, and a root beer."

"I'll get Henry right on it."

Lucas looked around the small diner and was relieved to not see anyone he knew. A few minutes later Christy came back with his food. He took his time eating. After a while Christy came by with a slice of peach pie without him even having to order it. It was warm, topped with one scoop of vanilla ice cream and a touch of honey.

After finishing his pie, Lucas looked up at the clock, which read 1:14 pm. It was time to head over to the doctor's office. He didn't want to be late for his appointment.

He handed Christy a $100 bill and told her to keep the change. She protested that it was too much, but he insisted that she take it anyway.

He grabbed a copy of the town's free weekly magazine out of a rack before leaving the diner. He then walked across the parking lot to the medical center and entered Doctor Pilter's office. The receptionist greeted him as he walked up to the counter.

"Hi Mister Fosterman. Are you here for your two o'clock appointment?" she asked.

"Hi Mary. I am early, but don't mind me. I wanted to get out of the heat for a while, so I thought I would borrow your air conditioner and read the paper."

"You can have all the AC you want, Mister Fosterman," she said with a smile. "We have one appointment ahead of you, so it shouldn't be long."

He sat quietly reading for about ten minutes before he saw the silhouette of a man appear at the door. He quickly raised the paper to hide his face and watched as a tall, middle-aged man with dark brown hair and a scraggly beard stepped through the door. He was wearing jeans and a blue button up work shirt that had Jim's Auto Repair embroidered just above the left pocket. He walked up to the counter where Mary was sitting.

"Hi, Jim Powers, I have a 1:30 appointment," he said in a voice that was much too soft for a man of his size.

"Yes Mister Powers, you are right on time. Why don't you go on back to Room 2 and the doctor will be with you in just a few minutes."

The man walked down the hallway and turned into the second door on the left. Lucas put down the paper and closed his eyes. Until now he had stayed calm, but his heart had started to race the second the man appeared in the doorway. He squeezed his eyes shut and rubbed them in an effort to keep calm. He took a couple deep breaths and counted to ten.

Finally, he felt steady enough to stand up and walk over to Mary. He could see that she was on the phone so he just waved and pointed down the hall toward the restroom. She shook her head in agreement and turned back to her appointment book.

Lucas continued down the hall, passing the restroom. He peeked into the room on the right and saw that it was empty. He also paused at the junction of a second hallway to see if anyone was around. The whole area looked vacant to his relief. He walked a little bit further stopping just two feet in front of Room 2. He took another deep breath and put his hand on his right hip.

Lucas walked into the room, closing the door behind him and locking it. Jim Powers sat on an exam table looking down at his phone, not really paying much attention. He looked up slowly and adopted a confused expression.

"You're not Doctor Pilter," he said as he put the phone down by his side.

Lucas turned toward the man with his 1911 pistol already pulled and ready. The man's eyes widened when he saw the gun. He instinctively held his hands out in front of his chest. Lucas didn't hesitate. He fired two loud shots directly into the man's belly. Jim jolted back on the table and clasped his hands over his stomach.

Lucas grabbed a chair and placed it under the door handle to block anyone from entering. He grabbed another chair and sat down directly in front of the man. Screams echoed from outside the room.

"Do you know who I am, Jim?" Lucas said with no malice in his voice.

"No! No!" The man screamed. "Why the hell did you shoot me!"

"My name is Lucas Fosterman. I am Katie's grandpa," Lucas replied. "Now do you understand?"

The man started sobbing and looked down at the large blood stain that began to soak through his shirt and pants. He knew he was going to die.

"I need you to understand that I have forgiven you for what you did to our little Katie. It was not easy and it took time, but I found a way to forgive you. This is not about vengeance. It is not about hate or retribution. I need you to understand that. This is about helping my family find peace and salvation. I need my son Mark and Katie's mother Lisa to let go of their hate for you. I need to make sure my son Paul doesn't do something that will land him in prison for the rest of his life. I need Katie's brother to build a life for himself that is not filled with guilt and resentment. I need for all my loved ones to start remembering Katie as she was and not think about you every time they see an image of her. You see, I am doing this for my family. I am doing this so that they can find their own paths to forgiveness."

Once Lucas had said his piece, he watched Jim sob a little longer before his arms went limp. A few seconds later he noticed that his chest stopped heaving. Lucas watched as his pupils dilated.

The pistol was still in his hand. He released the magazine and removed the bullet from the chamber. He left the slide locked back to show that the weapon had been cleared and placed it on the ground. He stood up and moved his chair aside, then pulled the other chair out from beneath the handle and unlocked the door. He pulled out his cell phone and dialed his old golf buddy Greg.

"Hi Greg. I am going to have to cash in a favor today. Can you meet me down at the police station in about an hour? It should not take long… Thanks Greg. See you then."

He unlocked the door and walked to the back of the room where he knelt down on the ground and waited for the police to arrive.

The Civility of it All

The whole process from that point was fairly mundane. The police rushed into the doctor's office ready for war, but instead found a serene old man kneeling with his hands behind his head. The first two officers through the door recognized Lucas. They also recognized Jim Powers.

It took very little effort for the officers to figure out what had happened. They stood Lucas up and put him in handcuffs. As they led him out the front door, Lucas could see Doctor Pilter and Mary looking at him in disbelief. Across the way, Christy and Henry also stared at the scene in stunned amazement.

Lucas was driven to the police station where he was read his rights, processed, and eventually placed in an interrogation room. Greg showed up a few minutes later and rushed into the room. He was ready to mount a vigorous defense. He started citing things like temporary insanity, self-defense and justifiable homicide.

"Greg. Greg. It is okay. It is okay." Lucas said trying to calm him down. "Look, I did it. I knew what I was doing. I planned it out, and I am okay with what comes next. I will plead guilty. I will accept life without parole. I do not want a trial. I do not want to go through the sentencing process."

"But Lucas, you deserve a defense," said Greg. "You have a

chance. I need to defend you."

"Greg, what I need from you is to make sure that this does not go to trial. That is all. I am a tired old man. I just want to go to prison and get some rest. Can you do that for me?"

"Lucas, I don't understand…" Greg began, but he quickly realized that it was hopeless. "I know you well enough to understand that you have made up your mind. I will do what you ask."

A few minutes later the district attorney walked in the room. He was in his mid-forties, wore a decent suit, and had perfect attorney hair. He took a seat across from Lucas and Greg and looked up at Lucas with sad eyes.

"Mister Fosterman, your family has had more than its share of tragedy these past several years. I hate to be part of heaping on more pain, but you have forced my hand here."

"It is alright son. I plan to make this as easy as possible for everyone involved," said Lucas. "What are your terms?"

"Based on what I know so far; I am going to have to charge you with first degree murder. That would mean life without parole. Given your age, you would be sent to the Graybar Penitentiary's geriatric wing for the rest of your life."

"Well, I have never really thought of myself as geriatric, but if that is what the state wants to call me then so be it. I accept your terms."

"What?" Said the stunned prosecutor.

"I accept your terms. Where do I sign?"

That was it. Lucas wrote out a short confession, signed a few documents, and the deal was done. He had to stand before a judge and profess his guilt, but Greg made sure that was all done later that same night when no one was around.

He was already on the bus headed to Graybar Penitentiary before the sun came up the next morning. Even the media didn't get the story until after he had been processed and was sitting in his new home in Cell Block D.

Visitor's Day

Mark Fosterman sat in his red work truck in the visitor's parking lot at the prison.

It had only been two weeks since the shooting, but it felt like an eternity to him. He fully understood what his dad had done and even understood why he did it. He just couldn't believe that his father had gone through with it.

His father was the most loving man he knew. He wasn't quick to anger and had an abundance of forgiveness. He had even worked hard to convince Mark, Paul, and everyone else in the family to forgive that monster for what he did to Katie.

He couldn't believe that things had spiraled so out of control for his family over the past decade.

It had been nine years ago that Katie had gone missing from their neighborhood. She loved to ride her bike around their small subdivision. It seemed like a perfectly safe thing for any ten-year-old to do.

The worry turned to panic turned to gut-wrenching fear as the minutes turned to hours turned to days. Everyone in the family, the local FBI, the police, even the whole town, pitched in to help look for little Katie. The search went on for three days until someone found the body of a young girl in an abandoned barn just past the edge of town. It was the worst day of his life. Until then there had been hope.

Then came the painstaking investigation. The police ruled out Mark right away because he had been working at the showroom when his daughter went missing. The showroom had cameras, plus his dad and brother had been with him the whole time. They had been working long hours that week in preparation for the Fall Festival.

Lisa wasn't as fortunate. She had been home being a good mother, but that didn't provide for much of an alibi. She was forced to endure three hours of questions and speculation. She was broken when they found Katie, and a few hours of interrogation widened the cracks. The lab reports eventually ruled her out. But that was a hollow victory because the reports also confirmed another horror... Katie had been raped. Lisa was shattered. She stayed in bed for over a week and wouldn't talk to anyone.

The small-town police were not accustomed to dealing with such a high-profile case. They brought in more than a dozen "suspects," all of whom were on various predator lists. They were eager to make an arrest to help calm the community, but they forgot all about due process. They questioned people even after they asked for lawyers. They tried to coerce confessions. They even took DNA samples without warrants or legitimate cause.

Jim Powers was one of the men brought in with the original group of potential suspects. As the investigation proceeded, signs started to point to him. The evidence was overwhelming. The barn turned out to belong to his uncle. His DNA was found on Katie. During the investigation, he slipped up and revealed details about Katie's dress that only the killer would know. It should have been a slam-dunk case.

In the end, the case was thrown out during the discovery phase. The DNA evidence linking Jim to Katie was obtained illegally, and the interrogation was deemed inadmissible due to coercion. At that point, the District Attorney's Office had no choice but to drop all charges. They promised to keep the case open until they could gather more evidence, but everyone knew it was hopeless.

Mark was outraged. Tyler was outraged. Paul was homicidal. Lisa was suicidal. It was Grandma Sarah that kept everyone together. She convinced them to let things play out in the court system a little longer before making any rash decisions.

A few weeks later, Jim Powers was taken into custody on a

different assault and battery charge. Apparently, he had beaten up some woman who was staying with him. This was his second felony offense, and he was eventually sentenced to a minimum of eight years in the state prison. This gave the family some time to heal and put their lives back together.

The first six months after Jim was locked up were still hard. Tyler left for college and Lisa completely checked out of the family. She moved in with a girlfriend of hers, leaving Mark alone in the house. The rest of the family slowly got back to living their lives. But the hate and pain didn't go away.

Eventually, Lisa would file for divorce. Mark and Paul threw themselves into building and selling furniture. Lucas and Sarah started planning for retirement.

When Sarah died, it was another blow to the family. She had found a lump on her left breast one day and less than a year later she was gone. It was hard on Lucas. He spent most of his days at the shop making furniture. He poured his love for his late wife into making an amazing amount of beautiful pieces. The showroom quickly filled up, and they had to expand the floor space to accommodate the growing inventory and volume of new customers. Eventually, Lucas slowed down and started training his sons and a few trusted employees on how to build his designs. This allowed him to relax a bit and start thinking about retirement again.

One Christmas Lucas gifted both his sons with legal documents granting them fifty-fifty ownership in the business. Mark and Paul insisted that Lucas take a monthly "severance" check, and he reluctantly agreed.

Mark smiled as he remembered how excited he and Paul were to start running the shop together as owners. He felt a twinge of guilt for smiling after all that had happened, but he knew his dad would approve.

He took a deep breath and shut off the engine. He didn't know if he was ready to see his father behind bars, but he really didn't have a choice. He climbed out of the truck and started the long walk to the visitor's entrance.

Father and Son

Mark sat in the uncomfortable waiting room along with about twenty other people.

He had spoken to his dad for about two minutes three days ago, but that conversation was all about making Mark promise to come to the first visitor's day alone. Otherwise, his dad hadn't spoken with any of the other family members since the shooting.

The heavy metal prison door slid open and the prisoners were allowed to walk through, one at a time. Lucas was the seventh one through the door, and he smiled when he saw Mark.

Mark was taken aback by how healthy and peaceful his dad looked. For some reason, he expected him to look tired and weary. Instead he was clean shaven with combed hair and what could only be described as a spring in his step.

They gave each other a quick hug and sat down at the table.

"How have you been? How are Paul and Tyler and Lisa and everyone else?" Lucas asked.

"We are all doing fine. Everyone is worried about you."

"Do not worry about me. I'm good. I have tons of books to read, and they let me sleep as much as I want. I never thought I would be so happy to be considered a geriatric." Lucas smiled.

"Dad, I don't know what to say... Everyone is shocked. Everyone in town is proud of you. Hell, I'm proud of you—"

"Now stop right there," Lucas said cutting him off. "There is nothing for anyone to be proud of. I committed a sin by killing that man. No amount of justification can change that fact. I did not do it out of malice or hate. I did it because I needed to find a way for everyone in the family to move on. And I guess I needed to let go too.

"Somehow, I think I blamed Jim Powers for your mother's death. She put on a brave face for the family, but I think her spirit was broken when Katie died. That is why the cancer took her so quickly. It may not make sense medically, but I guess I had to blame someone. It might as well have been Jim Powers.

"But all of that is over now. I just do not want anyone thinking I am some kind of hero. I know what I did was wrong and everyone else knows it too. I will live out my last days in prison, as it should be, and maybe I can find some way to do some good in this place."

"Dad, we can appeal this. We can fight this. I talked to Greg and he said he has a plan."

"That is nonsense. I forbid Greg or anyone from appealing my case. I made a deal with the district attorney, and I am going to stick by that agreement. Besides, I really feel like I belong here right now. I need you to honor my wishes on this, and make sure everyone else in the family does as well."

Mark slumped back in his chair and reluctantly nodded his agreement.

"Now on to business," Lucas said leaning in. "Do you remember the first place you ever smoked a cigarette? Do not say anything, just nod yes or no."

Mark nodded yes shooting his dad a curious look.

"I need you to visit that place when you leave here. I left something there for you, Paul, and Tyler. Don't worry it is nothing bad. It is just a small gift to make up for all the Christmases and birthdays I am going to miss down the road."

Mark started to ask a question, but decided it probably wouldn't be a good idea. He knew his dad well enough to tell that there was more to the story.

After a few moments of silence Lucas broke the tension, "So tell me about Tyler. How is he doing with the new girlfriend?"

The two men talked for another forty-five minutes about family, friends, and work. Finally, the bell rang signaling the end of visitation time. The big heavy metal door slid open again, and the guards started ushering prisoners back to their cells. Lucas gave Mark another hug before heading through the doorway.

Mark was a bit numb after the visit with his dad, and he drove back to town in a bit of a fog. He made it all the way into town before remembering the "mission" that his dad had sent him on. He thought about going to pick up Paul before heading out to the old farmhouse, but decided he would check it out on his own first.

He turned left at the first light in town, and headed out P Highway. The farmhouse was only about nine miles out of town, and he still had plenty of daylight left.

Three Boxes

Mark drove up to the old, run-down farmhouse. He had inherited the farmhouse and the surrounding seventy acres from his grandmother as his share of the family's large hog farm that hadn't been in operation for more than thirty years.

He jumped out and walked around to the back of the house. He could see the old tin cellar doors laying on the ground with a combination lock securing the rusted latch. He set the numbers to 0208 for the months he and Paul were born. The lock snapped open and he pulled back the heavy doors.

As he walked down the narrow concrete stairs he chuckled a bit remembering the first time he had gone down those steps.

He had been only seven at the time, and he had found a pack of unfiltered Camels and a box of matches sitting next to his grandpa's tractor seat. He thought he was old enough to give them a try, so he snuck away to the cellar and pulled out a cigarette. Not knowing he needed to suck on the end, it took him three matches to finally light the cigarette. He put the cigarette up to his lips and breathed in a solid drag. The pain and shock of the horrible puff forced him to drop the cigarette and start to cough violently. The cigarette landed in a patch of dried leaves, which quickly caught fire. The panic was immediate, and he started shouting and pushing on the closed cellar doors. The smoke grew thick in a matter of seconds, and his eyes teared up and started to sting. He banged on the doors in desperation and yelled for help. His father threw open the cellar doors, grabbed him by the arms, and yanked him out. A few stomps later and the fire was gone.

He could still remember sobbing uncontrollably and just saying "I'm sorry! I'm sorry!" over and over again. After his dad calmed down, he came over and hugged him and told him it would be okay. "We all do stupid things sometimes. That's how we learn to stop doing stupid things."

Mark reached the bottom of the stairs and felt around on the wall for the light switch. The light was blinding at first. It took a few seconds for his eyes to adjust, but he could see the shape of an old workbench start to come into focus.

He was immediately drawn to the three boxes that sat on the center of the workbench. He approached them in stunned silence. They were absolutely beautiful, a cross between small treasure chests and manly-looking jewelry boxes. Each box was about two-feet wide by a foot deep. They were adorned in ornate hinges and latches. The carvings were exquisite and clearly represented the finest woodwork he had ever seen.

It was immediately evident that the boxes were designed for himself, Paul, and Tyler. Everything from the type of wood to the color of the stain to the hardware to the intricate carvings spoke to each of their preferences. Mark could see a detailed carving of his high school and university crests. A band of fleur-de-lis surrounded the lid, a nod to his favorite football team. The rich brown oak had always been his wood of choice. The antique brass hinges, latch, and pad lock were exactly what he would have chosen, if he could have even found such exquisite pieces. Every carving, every small detail, had been taken into consideration.

Mark took his time going over each box in great detail. He just kept shaking his head and muttering to himself. "These are utterly amazing. They must have taken months to complete. Dad, you have really outdone yourself. This is by far your finest work."

Next to the workbench stood a tall, wrought iron stand holding a metal ring containing three ornate keys. Mark found the key that matched the lock on his box and unlocked it. He opened the lid and gasped a bit. It contained bars and coins of gold and silver... and lots of it. He couldn't even guess at how much it must be worth. On top of the precious metals sat an envelope with his name on it. He opened it and read the short letter.

Take these boxes and store them away somewhere safe. Preferably not at your house and not at the showroom. I converted everything I own into gold and silver and divided it into these three boxes for you boys. I do not know what the future holds for me, but I did not want to give Jim Powers' family a reason to bring a civil case against me. I figured this was the safest way to ensure I left something behind.

Each box contains around $500,000 worth of precious metals, so keep them secure. When you feel it is safe, use the money for whatever you want. Buy a car or a boat or a house. Take a cruise around the world. Give it to charity or just bury it in your backyard for a rainy day. The choice is yours, as long as you spend it on something for yourselves. I do not need anything anymore.

I am content knowing that you boys can move on and forgive that monster for taking away our precious Katie. You must forgive him now and go on living good lives. The evil that took her away from us has been removed from this world. Now you can get your hearts right and remember Katie as the sweet child that she was. She is sitting in Heaven now with your mother. My actions may not allow me to join them in the end, but it will be worth it if I have helped in some way to pave a path to your future salvation.

Take care of one another and love one another.

Your Loving Father

Mark wiped away a few tears as he put the letter back in the envelope. He closed his box and sat down on a small wood chair staring up at the three boxes. He knew his father was right. They could finally move on. For the first time in nearly a decade he allowed the weight of the world to go, he allowed his hate to float away. He sat down on a small wooden crate, bowed his head, and began to pray. It was the first time he had prayed since they had found Katie.

A Solitary Cell

In the geriatric wing there were only single bunks and most cells housed just one inmate at a time. Lucas figured that the government believed that old timers had experienced a lifetime of human contact and would be better off left alone.

The irony of his situation crossed his mind. He had spent much of his early adult life in the military guarding prisoners, and now he would live out the end of his adult life as one of those prisoners.

He sat on the bunk recalling the events of the past two weeks. He hadn't really taken the time to process everything until now. His time and energy had been filled with in-processing, adjusting to life in prison, and finishing out his family obligations.

After meeting with Mark on visitor's day, he felt like he had completed his journey. All that was left for him to do now was to find a way to be useful in his new home and begin making amends for his transgressions.

A loud bell sounded, signaling lights out. Lucas laid back in his bunk and closed his eyes. As he tried to drift off to sleep, he saw a familiar image. The image of Jim Powers with his shocked expression, dilated pupils, and blood soaked shirt filled his mind. He could see it all in vivid color. He knew there was no use trying to block it out. The image appeared every time he shut his eyes, and he doubted that it would ever go away.

Prison Life – Year One

"The hottest love has the coldest end."

– Socrates

Happy Anniversary

Lucas had been standing in front of the calendar in the prison woodshop for several minutes. He was the first person to enter the shop, so he took the liberty of flipping the calendar page from April to May. That's when it hit him – he was just a few days away from reaching his first full year as a prisoner.

"That must be one pretty tractor, Fosty," said a familiar gruff voice using Lucas' prison nickname.

Lucas turned around to see Elwood Martin starting to pull cans of stain and varnish out of the supply locker.

"I've always been partial to John Deere green."

"I guess it's been about a year for you. I suppose I can't call you fish anymore." Elwood smiled.

Elwood had been Lucas' friend and mentor for the past year. The eighty-year-old man was a seven-year prison veteran. Elwood had taken Lucas under his wing and helped him adjust to prison life. Lucas owed the man a lot.

The two men lived in adjoining solitary cells, which allowed them the opportunity to have countless hours of conversation. It had only taken them a few weeks to become good friends, and after several months, they knew more about each other than people they had known for decades.

Elwood had learned about Lucas' family, his past, and the events that landed him in jail. They had spoken for long hours about why Lucas felt he needed to kill Jim Powers and about how he was conflicted over his actions. Elwood had listened to Lucas shift between periods of guilt and attempts at justification, sometimes within the same conversation.

Lucas knew all about Elwood, his lovely wife Grace and their grown daughter Patricia. He knew how much he missed Grace, and how he longed to get back to her as soon as his sentence was over. Lucas knew Elwood was a good man, who had made a dumb mistake.

Elwood had always been a bit of a drinker, especially in his younger days. He had gotten a couple DUI's in his twenties, but he had grown up a lot after getting married and having a daughter. It only took one bad decision to change all that. He had met up with friends for a monthly card game. Elwood had downed a few more drinks than usual that night, but he still felt sober enough to drive home. He never completed the five-mile trip home. Instead, he veered into the wrong lane and smashed his SUV into a small sedan killing a young mom and her son. He was convicted of vehicular manslaughter and sentenced to ten years.

Most of the inmates living in the geriatric wing of Graybar Penitentiary were assigned to library duty or janitorial work, but because of Lucas and Elwood's years of woodworking experience, they were assigned to help teach younger prisoners how to make rocking chairs, footlockers and other basic pieces of furniture.

Lucas was still in solid physical condition and found it easy to shape wood using the shop's large collection of antiquated tools. Making simple rocking chairs and even more mundane footlockers required only a fraction of his advanced skills, but he was excited to have any opportunity to work with wood.

Elwood, on the other hand, suffered from arthritis. His shriveled and boney hands couldn't grip tools for more than a few minutes and his poor eye sight made it hard for him to accurately measure and cut boards. Still, he was a master at mixing stains to enhance the beauty of any piece of wood.

The two men spent their days training and working with the twelve other prisoners assigned to the woodshop. Most weeks, the crew could complete either twenty rocking chairs or forty footlockers, depending upon what their order sheets specified.

Since today was Friday, the men were completing the inspections on twenty rocking chairs that were set to go to market. Lucas completed the first round of inspections pointing out areas that needed a bit more sanding. Elwood followed behind touching up the stain before giving the green light for other prisoners to start applying lacquer.

By noon, the crew had finished the final touch up work and were led to the mess hall for lunch. Lucas and Elwood, being old-timers, were allowed to go through the line first. They sat down and started eating what looked like some sort of meat patty.

After just a few minutes, Warden Buckman walked through the main doors and motioned for the lead guard. The two men spoke for a while looking in the direction of where Lucas and Elwood were sitting. They continued speaking as they walked over to the table.

"Mister Martin, can you please come with me," said the warden in a stern but polite tone. The words caught Lucas off guard. The warden almost always called prisoners by their first names, and he was not a man who used the word please very often. Plus, there was a look on the man's face that made him feel uneasy.

Lucas could tell that Elwood was thinking the same thing as he stood up and held out his hands to be cuffed. It was procedure for a prisoner to be cuffed before being taken to the administrative wing.

"There won't be any need for that Elwood," said the warden. "Just follow Jerry; I will be along in a second."

The woodworking crew watched as Elwood was led out of the mess hall. The warden turned to Lucas. "How is everything going with this week's order?"

"Everything is ready boss. We are just waiting for the final clear coat to dry."

"Very good. The truck should arrive soon, and I will need you to supervise the load up without Elwood this afternoon."

"No problem, boss. We will get it loaded up. Should we include the custom order in the shipment?"

"No, just leave that one in woodshop and I will take care of it later."

With that the warden walked away leaving the men to speculate as to what was going on with Elwood. The younger prisoners turned to Lucas for answers, but all he could do was shrug his shoulders.

An Easy Afternoon

By the time the crew returned to the shop, the box truck was already backed up to the loading dock and ready to receive the shipment.

Lucas stood at the edge of the loading dock as the younger prisoners started grabbing rocking chairs. He inspected each chair one final time before allowing the workers to load it on the truck.

After the truck departed, the crew set to work cleaning up the shop. All the tools had to be tagged and placed back into their racks and boxes. The heavier equipment had to be cleaned and lubricated. Every surface and floor had to be scrubbed clean and prepared for a new round of work to begin Monday morning.

As the younger prisoners went about their chores, Lucas turned his attention to the one lone rocking chair left in the room. It was finely crafted rocker that was made of beautiful oak. Lucas had spent two weeks sculpting the seat, back, arms, and spindles. He had also spent several hours carving intricate flowers throughout the piece.

Elwood had led the staining process on the piece, and both men spent an entire day applying a two-stage stain. They started with rich red, followed by a dark brown that was lightly wiped down to create a finish of beautiful red and brown swirls. Four coats of varnish helped to bring out the details on all the carvings.

Lucas spent over an hour fine sanding the carvings one last time before applying a last coat of lacquer. Once finished, he sat down with a bottle of water and admired the fine piece of furniture. He was proud of what he and Elwood had created. They did not often have the opportunity to work on custom pieces, and this was by far the best item they had crafted together.

Thinking about Elwood made him wonder what was going on with his friend. The warden did not make many appearances in the mess hall, and it was even more rare for prisoners to be taken out and led to the administrative offices. The whole situation left him with an odd pit in his stomach.

A Long Goodnight

Lucas had gone through dinner and library time without seeing or hearing anything about Elwood. He had racked his brain trying to think about what was going on. Maybe his lawyer had forced a meeting, maybe he was getting transferred, or maybe something had happened at home. There were only a few reasonable explanations, and not many of them were good.

As he returned to the geriatric ward, he could see that Elwood was now sitting on the bunk in his cell. The warden, a guard, and another man were talking to him behind the bars of the closed cell door. The men finished their conversation as Lucas approached, and the guard ordered Lucas to stand out of the way as the three men walked by.

The warden nodded hello to Lucas, but his attention was focused on the new man. Lucas did not recognize the man, but he did notice that he was wearing a suit and a white collar. This gave Lucas pause because he knew that Elwood was a Methodist, one of the few Protestant religions where the leaders often wore white collars.

Lucas waited until the men reached the end of the hall before walking over to Elwood's cell. The old man was still sitting on his bed, his head hanging low. Lucas didn't say anything at first. He was hoping to see his friend's face first to gauge the situation.

Finally, he decided to engage. "What is it Elwood? Is everything okay?"

"Not right now, Fosty. Maybe later." His voice was soft and low.

Lucas was about to try again when the bell sounded signaling time to line up for evening roll call. Lucas walked a few paces over and stood on the white line in front of his cell. He looked over at Elwood's cell and watched as he shuffled up to the line, still looking down.

Lucas waited until the second bell sounded and walked backwards into his cell. He tried to catch a sideways glance at his friend, but he was still looking down and away.

The lights dimmed throughout the cell block and Lucas lay in his bed worried. About an hour passed before he heard a small voice call out.

"Hey Fosty, do you still think about that guy you shot?"

The question caught Lucas off guard. "Sure Elwood. I think about him every night. I wish I didn't, but I just can't help it."

"That's good Fosty," whispered Elwood. "It's just God's way of reminding you that you did something wrong. I know you did it for a good reason, but that still doesn't make it right. But I'm sure you've worked all that out by now. You're a smart man."

The conversation was starting to worry Lucas. "What is going on Elwood? What happened today?"

"We can talk about that later Fosty," Elwood let out a long sigh. "Would you mind telling me the story of how you met your wife again?"

Lucas didn't understand, but he knew that his friend was sad and probably hurting inside. He knew whatever the news was, it couldn't be good. If it helped even a little bit, he was happy to talk about how he met his beautiful wife Sarah.

"Sure buddy. I don't mind at all."

Lucas started telling the story of how a young Marine stationed at a Naval Station just north of Seattle met the most amazing woman. Elwood listened intently for a while, smiling at some of the funny parts, even though he knew they were coming.

He waited until he heard Lucas describe a strong, confident young lady in a pretty black dress. He could hear the joy in his voice as he continued to describe that first encounter. But that joy was lost on Elwood.

Elwood reached into a small hole in the corner of his mattress and pulled out a three-inch piece of soft ash that he had smuggled out of the woodshop. The small piece of jagged wood had a sharp edge and just enough of a handle to make it work as a shiv.

He grabbed the corner of his wool blanket and stuffed it into his mouth. Biting down hard, he stabbed the edge into his wrist. It took every ounce of grip his arthritic hand could muster not to drop the makeshift knife. He had to twist the blade in a painful circle before it finally broke through the artery.

Now that the deed was done, he laid back on the bed and listened to Lucas as he continued his story. He let his arm hang down by his side as the blood poured out in pulsating streams. He tried to focus on Lucas' voice wanting to hear the end of the story, but it was no use. He no longer had any Grace in his life.

Columbus Day in Tacoma

"We are never so defenseless against suffering as when we love."
– Sigmund Freud

Fall 1961

***

Columbus Day is one of those odd holidays that only the government seems to acknowledge. It's hard to understand why the government clings to such a ridiculous notion. It is widely known that Mister Columbus was not the first pale-faced foreigner to set foot on the Western side of the world. Drunk Vikings, and probably a host of other wayward travelers, had already stumbled upon the "New World" years before. But since the European establishment had paid for his trip, the powers that be decided to name Columbus the Grand Discoverer.

It's not hard to imagine what the Native Americans must think of such an obviously racist holiday. At one time their ancestors had been sitting peacefully near the shore growing corn and smoking tobacco when the white man arrived. Declaring the original inhabitants to be savages and therefore not really human, they claimed the country in the name of the queen. To celebrate the taking of their land, the murdering of thousands of their family members and the crushing of their traditions, the Native Americans are allowed to join in on a peaceful day off from work the second Monday in October every year. At least the ones that work for the government.

***

A Beautiful View

It was 3 pm on Columbus Day and Fosterman was drinking Chianti at a high-rise hotel bar in Tacoma, Washington. It was a lovely hotel that housed a fancy bar on the 28th floor. The bar featured an open-air patio that had a scenic view of downtown Tacoma with the waterfront in the background.

The patio was small, but the inside of the bar was roomy with plenty of cushy couches, fabric lined walls, cherry wood tables and a polite, attentive bartender. A classy joint.

Lucas was feeling content with himself as he waited patiently for his friend Brandon to arrive.

Sipping peacefully on his large goblet of fancy red vino, he watched the Navy ships pass by the harbor on their way to exotic lands full of brown skinned women with smallish breasts and healthy appetites for young American boys. He would probably end up on one of those ships someday, but not in the immediate future.

Lucas was in Tacoma enjoying the first day of a seventy-two-hour pass. He was scheduled to ship off to mainland Japan on Tuesday, and his commanding officer had given him off the holiday weekend to pack up and say his goodbyes.

For the past three years, he had served in the military police detachment at Naval Station Everett. Being one of only a dozen Marines on a Navy base had been a unique experience. Policing unruly Sailors and running the drunk wagon on the weekends had made developing friendships a bit tricky. Still he felt the duty had gone well overall, and he loved spending time exploring all that Seattle, Tacoma, and the Puget Sound had to offer.

He had found out two weeks ago that he was being reassigned to some remote airfield in the southern part of mainland Japan that was about to be officially commissioned as a Marine Corps air station. He wasn't keen on leaving the country, but he knew it was better than being sent over to Vietnam to drudge through the swamps. Things had been smoldering in that part of the world for a while now, and it was likely to start flaming up sooner or later.

He was stirred from his thoughts by the sound of females. He didn't turn immediately, but instead tried to guess what he was in for. He heard several voices, all female, but there was something strange about the situation. As the voices grew louder it hit him. They weren't speaking English. Not German or Russian… Not French… Certainly not Chinese or Japanese…. Portuguese maybe? He knew some Spanish, which was similar. Not Portuguese he decided.

He gave up the game and turned to look at the group. It was breathtaking. There were at least six, no, nine girls swirling around the back corner of the bar. They were moving couches and chairs together, preparing to settle in.

They were all beautiful, and not in the normal all girls are pretty kind of way. These girls were honest to God beautiful. The whole lot was tall and thin. Too thin in same cases. Their hair was perfect. Their makeup, their clothes, their shoes... all perfect. They had perfect posture, perfect teeth... perfect everything. What were the chances that nine wonders would all converge in one bar at the same time?

"There're Prague models." The voice caused him to turn his head.

He looked over and saw Dean, the lone bartender, picking up his empty glass. Dean was in his sixties, a bit overweight with two adult kids, a mean wife, and he was a veteran of the Great War.

"You're kidding me." Lucas was stunned.

"No, sir. Prague models here for some sort of an event in the harbor."

Prague models? Lucas was sure that sort of thing was a myth. Something only found in the movies. But no, here he was the lone male sitting in a small bar in Tacoma looking at a gaggle of Prague models. Nine of them and no escorts in sight. It couldn't be that easy.

Lucas watched as the girls got situated and gave their drink orders. The whole affair seemed to take much longer than it should have. The language barrier may have been a factor, but the biggest delay came from the fact that each girl spent an inordinate amount of time studying the drink menu and asking questions. Dean stood patiently throughout the process, answering questions and scribbling down notes.

Finally ready, Dean headed back to the bar. This group was obviously high-maintenance, and it took the old bartender several minutes to make all nine drinks. His tray was filled with a collection of drinks featuring hues of pinks, blues, and greens.

There were even a few umbrellas and a chunk of pineapple. One glass of red wine stood out from the rest.

Dean delivered the order and quickly returned to the bar to grab Lucas another glass of Chianti. "Sorry about the wait."

"No worries. I'm just glad you still had some energy left to pour me a glass. That was an impressive show."

"Tell me about it," Dean sighed. "I haven't made most of those fancy cocktails in years."

"Why do the pretty ones always have to be so difficult?" Lucas grinned.

"It's been that way since the time of Adam my friend," offered Dean. "He would have never taken that apple if Eve had looked like a wrinkled bag of prunes."

Lucas chuckled and nodded his head in agreement. "Well, I guess I better figure out a way to infiltrate the pack."

"Buy one a drink."

"One? But…" Then it hit him. He's the only guy in the bar. Nine vain girls, one guy. "Dean, you're a genius."

He scoured the group looking for one that wasn't too skinny. He spotted a beautiful dark-haired princess wearing a simple black dress. Normally, he would go straight for a blonde, but he was feeling a bit exotic tonight. Plus, there was something about this girl.

She stood out among all the tall, light-haired stick figures. She looked somewhat innocent, but carried herself in a confident manner. The other girls were making obvious efforts to look disinterested, while constantly preening themselves. However, this girl was engaged in the conversations and made eye contact with whomever she spoke. She was definitely not a regular in the group.

"What's Cleopatra drinking?" Lucas nodded toward the group.

"Oh I see, the girl in the black dress. Nice choice. Red wine, house. She was the only one who ordered a reasonable drink."

"Why don't we go with Chianti. Maybe she'll be impressed with the big glass."

"Right away Mister Fosterman."

Trying to look inconspicuous, Lucas turned around and picked up a copy of the newspaper. He read the headlines. Oil prices up, stock market down... more people killing other people in the Pacific Rim.

A few moments passed and he looked back to see Dean carrying a tray holding a lone glass. He had to excuse his way past two tall blondes and a redhead to get to his target who was sitting near the middle of the group.

Lucas made sure he was turned to the side as the old bartender handed her the glass and gave a slight nod his way. He waited a few seconds before looking back. Most of the girls were trying to act coy, ignoring the new queen of the ball, who was blushing slightly and showing off her fancy new glass. The game was set.

He decided to let things stew a little longer before making his next move.

His eyes went back to the paper and more headlines. Yankees win the pennant. Another boxing scandal. Emerson and Lever are still on top in tennis.

Dean pulled Lucas' attention by handing him the phone. "It's the front desk."

Brandon was on the other line. "Where are you?"

"In the bar."

"Right then."

"Look, when you get here head straight for me on the balcony, understand."

"What the hell are you talking about?"

"Listen, there is a gaggle of the most amazing geese in this place. I'm saying don't look around, just head straight for the balcony. Got it?"

"Fine. Fine. Damn you're odd."

A few minutes later Brandon entered the bar. Lucas was the first to see him as he rounded the corner. He hesitated a bit upon seeing the girls... always the pervert. He quickly recovered and set a path to Lucas' position on the balcony. Eyes straight ahead.

Brandon was a rather imposing figure. He stood a couple inches over six-feet tall, bulky frame, broad shoulders, square chin, and youthful face. His hair was cropped short and he always wore black slacks and a tight black button up shirt – a regular Johnny Cash wannabe. He carried a serious, almost superior look, which turned to a menacing stare as he filled up with alcohol.

Lucas and Brandon had known each other since Marine boot camp and had even gone through MP school together. The two men had received identical orders to Everett three years ago and had stood watch together at the main gate for hundreds of hours.

Brandon's favorite duty had been working the drunk wagon where he got to knock the heads of drunken enlisted men, and especially officers, who had partied a little too hard out in town. About a year and half into their duty at Everett, Brandon let his temper get the best of him one night and slugged an overbearing Navy commander one too many times.

The combination of a high-ranking Navy officer with a broken nose, two black eyes, and a cut lip turned out to be a career ender. Brandon was quickly handed a bad conduct discharge and forced to find a new line of work. The bulky Irishman simply went back to his roots, loaded up his truck with a few tools, and drove around looking for brick laying jobs. It took him a few months to build up a small business, but just over a year later he now ran a small crew of masons who had steady work throughout Puget Sound.

 Brandon took a seat across from Lucas, facing the girls.

"My Lord! What a wonderful sight."

"Indeed. And they're all Prague Models."

"You've got to be Shitting me! I've never had Czech before."

"Look, I need you to do me a favor." Lucas stared intently at Brandon.

"Alright," he answered, barely listening to what Lucas was saying.

"See the dark-haired beauty sitting in the center holding the big glass of wine."

"Yeah. Cleopatra."

"Exactly. I need you to point over at her and mouth something like, 'that one?', but make it obvious."

"Right."

Brandon sat up sharply and craned his neck to peer at the pack. He then stuck out his arm and awkwardly pointed a finger. Rolling his eyes in false disgust Lucas turned, gave a quick look, and shook his head yes. Before turning back around, he saw that the ploy had worked. Several of the girls were looking back at them as they singled out one from the group.

Dean came back over to take Brandon's order. "Two fingers of Wild Turkey and a glass of water. Hold the peanuts and pretzels. Got to stay healthy."

"Now don't get shitty."

"What do you think the water is for?"

"I think you pissed off the redhead in the corner the most," Dean said. "I guess she's the leader. She works for some big Vodka company and pulls in more money than the rest of the girls. Your dark-haired girl is new, not a model, not even a foreigner. I think they said she was from Kentucky or something like that. Either way, you have stirred something up."

"What the hell's going on? What are you up to?" Brandon's confusion was almost comical.

"I just bought her a drink, that's all."

"Just her... Damn that's clever. No wonder they all look like someone stole their lollipops."

"All right then. Could we have a shot of tequila delivered to the redhead? There's no need to piss off the Queen Bee. I'll take one for the team."

"Yeah. I'm sure it's a big sacrifice." Dean shot back, smiling.

The drink was delivered. Brandon was a bit less coy about his intentions. He simply stared at the redhead as Dean made his way back to the two men carrying more drinks.

"Have fun boys." The barman winked as he went about his duties.

"Look sharp," Brandon ordered. "Big Red is headed our way."

She pushed her way through the group of girls, making a small scene. They all watched her as she crossed the bar and stepped onto the patio. She placed her hand on Lucas' shoulder as she passed by, making his left nut jump slightly.

"I not drink this alone." She stood over Brandon as a thick accent rolled from her tongue.

"Well that would just be rude," Brandon replied as he jumped up and grabbed his shot of whiskey. "To the wonderful city of Prague."

They both swallowed their shots. Big Red was clearly impressed with how easily Brandon downed his fat goblet of whiskey. He immediately motioned for another round and offered a seat to his new prize.

Introductions were made, and they now knew one Miss Ivana Svoboda.

Ivana was a severely self-assured woman in her late twenties, a few years older than Brandon and Lucas. It was clear that she knew that she was superior to both the young "boys" and made this known with her dismissive body language and a few snide comments.

Lucas just rolled his eyes and pushed back in his chair. He had never been one to abide rude people, no matter how beautiful they may be. Brandon, on the other hand, looked at the situation as a challenge and began reciprocating her rude behavior and dismissive manner.

"Look at the legs on that girl in the blue dress," he said to no one in particular.

Ivana took the bait, "They are okay, but she has big teeth and small feet."

"With legs like that why would anyone look at her teeth?"

Ivana got up and leaned over the railing a bit, pretending to look at the view of the city. She stood up on her tip toes, pushing out her butt in an obvious attempt to grab some needed attention. The ploy worked as Brandon ogled her perfect figure with wide-mouthed amazement. Even Lucas couldn't help but lift an eyebrow in approval.

Brandon gave Lucas a devious look and bit his knuckles. He jumped up from his chair and joined Ivana at the railing.

Lucas shifted a bit in his chair, turning away to give the two a little privacy. He looked back over at the group of girls and noticed that Cleopatra was no longer with the pack.

He scanned the rest of the small bar and saw that she was now sitting at the bar with Dean, who had just handed her the phone. He knew this was his chance. He gave her a few seconds to settle into her call before walking up to the bartender and asking for another drink.

Lucas sat just close enough to hear Cleopatra's conversation. "Okay Barbara. Well if you're not coming up, then I will just head to my room and get some work done. None of the decision makers showed up, just a bunch of their booth bunnies. I'll see you in the morning, and I hope you start feeling better."

She handed the phone back to Dean and thanked him. Buttoning up her purse, she looked over at Lucas. "Thank you for the drink. I hope you and your friend have a wonderful night." She looked over at Brandon, who was now following Ivana over to the group of girls.

Lucas was still looking back at Brandon when he noticed that the girl in the black dress was walking away. "Can I least get your name?"

"Sarah. Sarah Blackstone."

"I'm Lucas. Lucas Fosterman." He stuck out his hand to offer a handshake. It was an awkward move, and he immediately felt dumb.

Sarah shook his hand, and he was surprised by the firmness of her grip. For such a dainty creature, she had a better handshake than most of the guys he knew. "Nice to meet you Lucas Fosterman. And thanks again for the drink."

With that, Sarah turned and walked away. He thought about calling after her, but that would have made him look like even more of a goober.

Alone in the Crowd

It had been almost two hours since Sarah had left the bar, and Lucas had been sitting on a stool nursing his glass of wine. For some reason he couldn't get her out of his mind, even given all the other pretty distractions in the room.

He looked up to see Brandon howling with laughter. The tall Irishman was certainly in his element. One man, eight girls, and a pile of booze. He was in rare form telling stories of life as a "seasoned former Marine." His audience was hanging on his every word.

Brandon finished another one of his fairy tales and looked over at Lucas, giving him a scowl. Not getting a response he walked over.

"Stop sulking man. You always do this. You get fixated on the one girl you can't have. There is a world of possibilities in this room."

"I'm not sulking. I'm just tired. I spent all day packing up and checking out. I'll be better tomorrow."

"You better old man. We've only got a couple days left together before you head off to the rock. Go get some sleep, and I'll meet you tomorrow morning for breakfast. Reveille is at 8 am sharp, I want to get an early start on our road trip."

"Sounds good. Try not to get into too much trouble."

"I sure as hell am not going to make that promise!" Said Brandon as he jumped back into the ring of girls.

A Chance Meeting

Lucas was standing in the hotel lobby store holding a Coke and looking at the cigarette and gum rack. He was just about to make a selection when he heard a familiar voice. "I hear those things are supposed to kill you now."

He turned around to see Sarah Blackstone standing there. She still wore her black dress and was holding a newspaper and a Coke.

Lucas held up a pack of Double Mint gum in his defense. "You won't see me smoking those smelly things," he replied with a smile. "No matter how uncool that makes me."

"There may be hope for you yet Lucas Fosterman. She returned his smile. "So what made you abandon your mission at the bar? I thought you guys had a good shot at bagging a couple of those liquor bunnies. You had such a smooth entry onto the field, and your buddy was moving pretty quick with Ivana."

"Well, all the pretty girls left the bar." He grinned.

Sarah rolled her eyes and gave him a half-hearted look of disgust.

"All right. All right. I'll stop." Lucas chuckled. "I'm obviously not getting anywhere with my cheeseball moves."

The cashier rang up Sarah's Coke and newspaper. She grabbed Lucas' Coke and gum from him to add to the order. "I owe you for the drink."

"I don't think you understand how the whole guy hitting on a girl thing works." Lucas smiled. "I'm supposed to buy you stuff, and you are supposed to—"

"Supposed to what?"

"Supposed to smile and say thank you," he said, chuckling again. *Who was this girl?* "Are you always this grumpy."

"I'm not grumpy. You're the one who is offended by a girl buying you a Coke and pack of gum."

"Okay, you win. Here is your smile and thank you very much. Hey, does that mean that you just hit on me?"

"Don't press your luck!" She elbowed him in the ribs.

Entering the lobby, Lucas decided that he would press his luck and asked her if she wanted to take a seat at one of the little high-top tables. He was delighted when she agreed.

The two spent the next hour talking about the basics of their lives. It turned out Sarah was from a little town outside of Louisville, Kentucky. Her family owned the Blackstone Oak

Barrel Company, and she was in town for some sort of convention trying to sell barrels to liquor makers.

Her father had started the business in the 1940's. He recently suffered a mild heart attack, so Sarah had been asked to take his place at the convention this week. For years her father had been grooming her to take over the business, and he saw his bad health as an excellent excuse to force her out of her comfort zone.

Lucas also related a few stories about growing up in small town Missouri, his love for woodworking, and his decision to join the Marines three and a half years ago. He talked about how he enjoyed serving as a Military Policeman, but he knew it wasn't something he wanted to do forever. He desperately missed working with his hands and being creative. He also talked about his upcoming deployment to Japan where he would be spending the next year at a new air station.

After the ornate grandfather clock in the lobby chimed midnight, Lucas unwittingly let out a big yawn. Sarah instinctively followed with her own yawn, which made them both laugh. It was time to say goodnight.

"So, me and Brandon, that's the big Irish clod I was with tonight, we are planning to drive up through the Puget Sound tomorrow to visit some of the port towns. Nothing fancy, just a short road trip up and back. You're welcome to come along if you want."

Sarah looked down and shrugged. "I'm supposed to spend the day with my friend Barbara. But thank you for the offer... It was nice meeting you."

Lucas nodded. This time Sarah was the one who stuck out her hand. Lucas took it and was pleased to find that her grip wasn't as firm this time. It was an awkward end to a pleasant evening.

Good Morning Indeed

Lucas was already halfway through breakfast when Brandon showed up with Big Red in tow. He looked a bit ragged from the evening's festivities, but Ivana looked as polished as ever.

"I go to lady's room. Order me coffee." She didn't even make eye contact with Lucas.

"I see you had an eventful night."

"You have no idea! Brandon slumped back in his chair. "That woman can drink an elephant under the table. She must have a cast-iron liver. At least you look chipper."

"Well someone has to exercise moderation. I take it that Miss Sunshine is going to be joining us today."

Brandon shrugged. "I guess I invited her along sometime during the evening. She banged on my door at 8 am dressed and ready to roll. Hey, maybe I can see if she has a friend that would like to go with us."

Lucas had stopped listening. He was pretty sure that he had just seen Sarah walk into the hotel lobby and he was trying to catch another glimpse to be certain.

"So what did you end up doing last night? Did you really go to bed at 11 o'clock?"

Just then Lucas saw Sarah reappear in the lobby and she was looking around for something. "Oh nothing, I just had a Coke downstairs." He stood up and threw his napkin in the chair. "I'll be right back."

Lucas lost sight of Sarah as he made his way through the small restaurant. He was about to turn the corner to the lobby when Sarah, looking the other way, walked right toward him. He grabbed her shoulders before she ran into him, which startled her. She looked up at him in surprise.

"Oh, good morning. Sorry about that!" She appeared a bit sheepish. "Actually, I was hoping to run into you."

"Well how fortunate. Were you in need of more cheesy

pickup lines?"

"No," she laughed. "But I did want to see if your offer to tag along on today's trip was still good."

"The offer is still good. What about your friend Barbara?"

"She isn't feeling well, so she is going to hang out in her room today."

"We are just sitting down to breakfast if you care to join us?"

Sarah nodded and they walked over to the table. "Sarah, this is Brandon, and I believe you know Ivana."

"Good morning, Ivana. Nice to meet you, Brandon."

"Nice to meet you, Sarah. Brandon flashed Lucas a crooked grin. "Just a Coke, huh?"

Road Trip

They had only been on the road for thirty minutes and Lucas could see that Ivana was still fuming as she desperately worked to keep her hair in place.

It had taken Brandon more than a few minutes to convince the prissy model to climb into the passenger seat of his Willys CJ-5. The soft top was in place covering the roof, but the windows had been removed making it look rugged. The openness of the cab created a strong vortex of wind that seemed to be focusing all its might directly at Ivana's upswept bun.

Sarah was positively giddy about the prospect of riding in the green all-terrain vehicle. She was the first to climb into the jump seat in the back and quickly pulled Lucas in after her. Her hair was tucked up in a bun, but she wasted no time in pulling out a few pins allowing her locks to fall around her shoulders. She was ready for action before Brandon even started the engine.

Lucas had never been happier to be "stuck" sitting on the narrow bench seat. He had no choice but to snuggle up close to Sarah and even moved to put his arm around her shoulders.

The road noise caused by the vehicle's large tires and the

constant whistling of the wind didn't provide much opportunity for conversation, which suited Lucas just fine. He was thrilled watching Sarah enjoy the ride. She occasionally threw her hands in the air to feel the wind rush by and used the roll bars for support as she stood up while they crossed the bridge over the Tacoma Narrows.

After about an hour's drive, they pulled into their first destination. Port Orchard was a sleepy little water-front community parked on the Sinclair Inlet of the Puget Sound. The town was filled with numerous small shops, quaint restaurants, and picturesque marinas housing dozens of sail boats and fishing charters. A military shipyard sat just across the inlet showcasing some of the Navy's most impressive hardware.

Sarah wasted no time jumping out of the Jeep and running into one of the small dress shops next to their parking spot. Lucas was afraid to follow her for fear that she may have made a mad dash to the restroom. Brandon was busy trying to settle the prickly Ivana down as she threatened to call for a taxi to take her back to the hotel.

Sarah reappeared a couple minutes later carrying two wide-brimmed hats and a handful of hair pins. She let Ivana have her pick of hats, which immediately improved her demeanor. After a few minutes of primping, the two women looked like seasoned locals ready for a midday stroll.

Lucas and Sarah decided to start with a walk through the marinas to take a closer look at the boats. Big Red decided that she wanted to go shopping and Brandon was ordered to join her.

Lucas felt in his element walking with Sarah through the small town. She listened intently as he described the various characteristics of the Navy vessels that could be seen throughout the inlet. Three years in the area had also provided him with a decent knowledge of the sailboats, fishing charters, and other civilian boats tethered to the slips located throughout the marinas.

They spent a couple hours walking around town before finally making their way back to where the Jeep was parked. As they approached, they could see Ivana sitting outside at a small restaurant sipping from a glass of wine. Brandon was a few feet away from her, working to strap down a small mountain of bags and boxes to the rear of the Jeep.

Lucas asked Sarah to order him a Jack and Coke and he walked over to help Brandon with his task. Brandon was in the middle of a cursing tirade when he approached.

"Need some help?" Lucas smiled widely.

"Wipe that stupid grin off your face. Why do you always get the nice polite girls while I get stuck with the self-absorbed dragon queens?" the Irishman sputtered.

"You wouldn't be happy without at least a little drama in your life. Besides, she gives you a chance to work on that patience you always say you need to learn."

After the guys finished with the packing, they joined the girls for lunch. It turned out to be a mostly silent and slightly awkward affair. Lucas and Sarah exchanged a few knowing glances as they could tell that the chemistry was beginning to wane between their travel companions.

On to Port Townsend

By 3 pm they were back on the road heading toward Port Townsend on the northern edge of the Sound. After another hour and half of driving, they entered the southern end of town.

Brandon wasted no time pulling into the first bar that he saw. He jumped out of the Jeep and made a beeline for the door, not even waiting for Ivana or the others. Ivana shrugged her shoulders and followed her grumpy companion into the bar deciding that she could also use a drink.

Lucas looked back to see that Sarah had walked up to the railing by the pier and was looking out across the bay. "That's the Port Townsend Bay," he said joining her. "To the right there is where we drove up Puget Sound. The first island is Indian

Island. Next to that is Marrowstone Island. And the large area across the bay is Whidbey Island."

"It's beautiful," she said. "I really love all the Victorian architecture and giant evergreen trees. Some of them must be at least three-hundred feet tall."

"We both have one more day before we leave. Why don't we take a trip over to Whidbey Island tomorrow?" He offered. "There is a place there called Deception Pass, and it is just about the most beautiful place I have ever seen."

"I would like that." Sarah suddenly looked shy.

They decided to take a short stroll up the pier to take in the sites. Lucas' heart jumped a bit when he felt Sarah slip her hand into his. He laughed to himself as he realized that he was experiencing puppy love for the first time since high school.

They continued to walk hand-in-hand for a while as Lucas pointed out the few historic details he knew about the area. He realized that he was talking too much, but he was a bit flustered for some reason.

After a while they headed back to the bar and decided to check in with the others. Lucas held the door open for Sarah then followed her in. A quick survey of the scene gave Lucas pause.

The big open bar was filled with more than a dozen high-top tables, and a long wooden bar lined the right wall. A dense cloud of cigarette and cigar smoke hung like a fog in the room. An unorthodox odor of stale beer and sea water permeated the air and the concoction was strong enough to make Lucas' eyes water.

To the left was a large group of lumberjacks, maybe about twenty. Lucas could tell they were lumberjacks by their enormous size and the fact that they were all wearing long sleeve shirts even with the mild fall weather.

The center area was filled with a group of Native Americans. There were several Indian Reservations located throughout the area, and Lucas knew many of the inhabitants to be hard-drinking, hard-fighting men. The Native Americans in northern Washington weren't the svelte toned men featured in Western movies. This group was built more like bear wrestling, trunk dragging warriors.

To the right was a group of about a dozen sailors and an assortment of locals. The crowd featured a heavy male versus female ratio, and a person could almost smell the testosterone in the room.

Lucas spotted Brandon sitting at a table close to the bar guzzling a shot of what was sure to be whiskey. Ivana was sitting next to him holding a glass of wine. Surprisingly, she didn't look as bitter as Lucas expected.

Sarah and Lucas took a seat at the table. "Where did you two wander off to." It was obvious the Irishman had already imbibed several shots.

"We just took a walk down the pier," Sarah blushed. "This place is just so beautiful."

"I see." Brandon waved the bartender over. "I'll take a double Wild Turkey, another chardonnay for the lady, and—"

"I'll have a beer." Sarah interjected.

"Me too." Lucas quickly added.

Lucas could see that Brandon was fixated on something on the other side of the room in the center of the group of lumberjacks. There was a small crowd standing around in a circle, but he couldn't tell what was so interesting. He noticed that others in the bar were looking in that direction as well. A few seconds later, he heard a loud cheer and the crowd stepped back revealing a large woodsman sitting at the far side of the table kissing his right bicep in victory.

He could see a small wooden table with two barstools sitting on opposing sides. There were two handles built into the table and what looked like leather cushions on each side. It was an arm wrestling table he decided.

One look at Brandon told Lucas that he was gearing himself up for a round of competition in the near future. He leaned over to Sarah to give her a heads up regarding the situation.

A few minutes later, a tall young sailor with decent sized arms stood up and walked over to the crowd. He pulled out his wallet and laid down some cash on the table. The current champion gave him a nod and the military man sat down and prepared himself. The crowd tightened again and a few seconds later there was another cheer. The lumberjack had won again.

The drinks arrived and Brandon quickly grabbed his whiskey, "That lug hasn't lost a match since we came in here. He took down a couple axe swingers and a lot of swabbies. I'm just waiting for that big Indian over there to make a run at him."

As if on cue, a large Native American stood up and made his way to the table. Brandon quickly swallowed his shot, grabbed Ivana by the hand and ran in for a closer look.

To Lucas' surprise, he felt his arm jerk as Sarah pulled him out of his seat. "Come on, I want to see."

By the time the four of them reached the table, both men were already locking grips and getting ready to start. A small brunette with double-sided pigtails was sitting on the side of the small table serving as a referee. She made sure everything looked even then started the match. This time, the action lasted a bit longer. The Indian looked to have the stronger arm in the beginning, but eventually the lumberjack moved back to even and eventually pushed his arm down to gain the victory.

There was another cheer from the crowd, and the Native American stood up and slapped the table in disgust. He didn't even bother walking back to his table and just pushed his way out the front door. This caused the group of lumberjacks to erupt in laughter.

The champion started chiding the crowd looking for another victim. He started with the Native Americans, then the sailors. He even called out a few locals by name. He poked a little fun at Lucas, who showed him that his human-size biceps were not up to the task.

Finally, Brandon pulled out a $5 bill and laid it on the table. The axman gave him an incredulous look, but smirked his approval. He was willing to take Brandon's money.

Brandon was a large enough man. He had decent biceps and an overall bulkiness to him. Still, he was not nearly as large as the lumberjack who quite possibly could have been the great grandson of Paul Bunyan. His arms looked like tree trunks and his hands were the size of ham hocks sporting huge sausage-like fingers.

As Brandon rolled up his sleeves, it revealed his one possible advantage. He had been slinging bricks, cinderblocks, and mortar for well over a year, which had allowed him to develop Popeye-sized forearms. With his sleeves rolled up, the area from his elbow to his wrist was even larger than his biceps.

Ivana leaned in and gave Brandon a long kiss on the lips for good luck. The gesture was as much a surprise to Brandon as it was to the rest of the crowd. The two men then settled into their chairs and locked grips. The pig-tailed referee made sure they were even and started the action.

The lumberjack's smirk quickly faded as he realized he wasn't going to put this match away without a fight. For the first few seconds, the two men stayed almost even, neither man gaining much of an advantage. Brandon pursed his lips and stared straight ahead. He slowly started to roll his wrist inward and push down in a steady motion. The giant woodsman gritted his teeth and his face turned beet red. He struggled with everything he had, but Brandon was eventually able to wrench his hand down in victory.

The crowd was stunned. There was no immediate reaction, just silence. Brandon slumped back in his seat and let out a sigh as he rubbed his wrist. The group of lumberjacks suddenly looked ominous. They stared at the previous champion who looked like he might explode. Lucas prepared himself for an upcoming battle and pushed Sarah behind him for cover.

The large axman slammed his fists on the table and let out a hearty laugh. "Bring this man a drink," he roared. "I want to get him drunk and try that again."

Everyone let out a cheer and Brandon received several slaps on the back. Ivana jumped in his lap and gave him another big kiss.

They stayed at the bar for another two hours watching as

Brandon took down three more lumberjacks and a few sailors. He even took another run at his new best friend, with the match ending in another Brandon victory.

A Sudden Goodbye

Lucas had taken over as driver now that Brandon was in no condition to drive. He was barely in any condition to walk when they left the bar. He and Ivana were in the back of the Jeep making out. Apparently, Brandon's prowess as an arm wrestler had been quite the aphrodisiac, and she could not keep her hands off him.

Lucas was a bit relieved when he pulled into the driveway to Brandon's small house just outside of Gig Harbor. The plan was for Lucas to drop Brandon off and drive the girls and himself back to the hotel for the night. However, the Jeep had barely stopped when Ivana pulled Brandon out of the backseat. Still locked at the lips, Brandon gave a sideways wave as he was pulled toward the house.

Sarah let out a laugh, and Lucas shook his head. "I'm guessing they want some alone time. I think we should head back to the hotel, and I can pick Ivana up tomorrow."

The final leg back to the hotel only lasted twenty minutes. Lucas was happy to finally stand up and stretch his legs after the two-plus hour drive. As they walked through the long parking lot, Sarah took his hand. Again, his heart jumped. They were still walking hand-in-hand when they entered the hotel.

As soon as they entered the lobby a short blonde haired lady started running their way. "Sarah, Sarah... Thank goodness you're back."

"Barbara. I'm glad you're feeling better. Lucas this is my friend Barbara."

"What? Oh, yes. Hi. Look, Sarah, I'm so sorry. It's your dad. He had another heart attack. Your mother called. She wants you to come home right away. It doesn't look good."

"Oh no!" Sarah was already starting to tear up. "I have to get a flight. I have to pack. I have to get home."

"I packed for you. Your bags are in my car, and your plane leaves in just over an hour. We don't have much time. I will bring the car around. Just wait here. I will be back in a minute."

With that Barbara left Sarah standing there with Lucas. They were still holding hands, and he could feel her trembling. He grabbed the handkerchief from his pocket and handed it to her. She let go of his hand and wiped away the tears.

She looked up at him, but couldn't manage to say anything. Lucas was also at a loss for words, so he just wrapped his arms around her. She pushed her head into his shoulder and started to sob. They stood there for another minute locked in an embrace in the center of the lobby alone in the crowd.

Barbara came running back into the lobby and motioned to Lucas that it was time to go. He walked Sarah out to the car and watched as Barbara ran and jumped into the driver's seat. He waved the doorman away and opened the passenger side door.

Sarah was about to climb in when she turned and looked at him. "I'm so sorry! It was such a lovely day. I wish we could have had more time together."

"I know. You have to get home, and I have to leave for Japan… Maybe the fates will bring us back together some day."

She grabbed her clutch and opened the snap. She reached in and pulled out a business card. She felt silly handing it to him, but it was her only option at that moment. "Write to me while you're in Japan. And if you ever find yourself near Louisville, come see me."

She gave him another hug and a kiss on the lips. Then she jumped in the car.

He watched as the car slowly vanished from sight wandering if he would ever see his Cleopatra again.

Prison Life – Year Four

"It is not necessary that whilst I live I live happily; but it is necessary that so long as I live I should live honorably."

— *Immanuel Kant*

Early to Rise

Lucas was pulled from a deep sleep by the sound of his name. He couldn't tell if the sound was coming from a dream or an actual person. He sat up in his bunk and rubbed his eyes to clear away the cobwebs. As his vision came into focus he could see Warden Buckman standing in front of his cell.

He stood up and faced the warden, furrowing his brow in confusion.

"Sorry to wake you Lucas, but I need to have a word with you. Why don't you get dressed, and I'll have a guard walk you down to the administrative wing."

With that, the warden turned and walked into the darkness. A few seconds later a guard Lucas didn't recognize walked up to the cell. Lucas was not familiar with most of the guards on the night crew because they hardly ever messed with the prisoners in the geriatric wing after lights out. The guard turned his back as Lucas finished dressing. "Okay, boss. I'm ready."

The guard signaled for the control center to open the cell door. A few seconds later, a loud click sounded and the door rolled open. Lucas held out his hands, and the guard loosely snapped the cuffs into place. He moved Lucas in front of him as they headed down the hall.

Lucas was still groggy, but his adrenaline was starting to kick in. He wasn't sure what the warden wanted with him. He just knew that it couldn't be good. Plus, the warden's grim look worried him. Thinking of Elwood, Lucas said a quick prayer that everything was alright with his family. He had seen the warden visit several fellow inmates to deliver bad news from home. However, that news was always accompanied by a chaplain.

Lucas' heart was beating fast when they arrived at the warden's office. He was slightly relieved when he saw that the warden was alone in his office sitting behind his desk. No chaplain. Lucas could tell from the doorway that the warden was upset. In the bright lights of his office, he could tell that his eyes were red and puffy, like he had been crying.

Lucas started to get the sense that this visit might not be about him.

"You can take the cuffs off Simon. Why don't you wait outside while I talk to Mister Fosterman."

The guard took off Lucas' cuffs and sat him down in one of the chairs in front of the warden's desk. The large man tapped his night stick against Lucas' chair and gave him a stern look on his way out as warning not to cause any trouble.

Lucas sat in the chair looking at the warden, who was researching something on his computer. Nothing was said for nearly five minutes.

Lucas realized this was the first time he had really seen the warden up close under proper lighting. Prisoners were discouraged from making eye contact with the man, and there had been minimal reasons for the two men to interact over the years. The warden had made a few short visits to the woodshop in the past, and he spoke to the prison population on occasion, but those events were rare.

Warden Buckman was a black man in his late fifties. Everything about the man appeared to be a contradiction. He was formal in his interactions, but his overall look and posture were sloppy. A scruffy beard cropped his round face, which always displayed a serious look. He only wore loose-fitting suits paired with black tennis shoes. He was a man of few words from what Lucas could determine, and he had a reputation for being firm, but fair.

"I'm sure you are wondering what you are doing here," said the warden standing up. "As you can imagine, I am not accustomed to asking prisoners for favors. But I find myself in an awkward situation."

The warden's face puckered a bit and he turned around, facing away. Lucas wasn't sure, but it looked like the man might be crying.

"How can I help boss?"

"I know you lost your granddaughter some time ago," he said softly. "How did you get through such a horrible tragedy?"

"I do not believe I have set a very good example of how to be a grieving grandfather. My grief eventually led to a series of decisions that landed me in this place."

"I suppose you're right. Who knows where grief will take me," the warden hung his head low. "Lucas, I lost my granddaughter Jody this morning. My damn son-in-law ran a red light coming home from the park. She died instantly, along with her little golden retriever puppy."

The words spilled out of the warden in a slow monotonous stream. Once finished, he wiped his eyes.

"I am sorry for your loss. There are no words to describe how it feels to lose a granddaughter. You grieve yourself, but you still have to be strong for your child. It is an impossible situation."

The warden nodded in agreement. "My daughter was inconsolable, as you can imagine. All day, she poured out her grief crying and yelling until we convinced her to lay down for a while. Then this afternoon she came down from her bedroom all peaceful and calm."

"She just started talking about the funeral arrangements. She already had the music picked out, along with the preacher, and bible verses. She had every detail worked out. Hell, she had even started writing the obituary. That's when I asked her what I could do to help."

The warden stopped for a second and turned around. His eyes were redder than before, but he was more composed. "That's where the favor comes in, Mister Fosterman. You may remember that I asked you to make that rocking chair for me about four years ago. It was made of oak, and you carved in rows of the most beautiful flowers. I gave it to my daughter as a gift just before Jody was born. It is her favorite piece of furniture, and she rocked her little girl in it every night."

The warden paused again and put his hands on his desk to compose himself. Lucas finally understood what was going on, and his heart was hurting for the man.

"Boss, if you would be kind enough to let me work in the woodshop today and Sunday, I would be honored to build a coffin for your little Jody. I would just need some wood, fabric, and few pieces of hardware."

"I can't order you to do this Lucas. I can't pay you or offer you any kind of deal. I might be able to get you some extra benefits from the commissary, but that's about it."

Lucas shook his head. "No boss. I do not want any money, or deals, or special benefits. You would be doing me a favor by letting me complete this task for you and your family. I have a lot to make up for in my life, and this would be a way for me to find a small piece of redemption."

"Thank you, Lucas. Just let me know what you need, and I will get it for you. I will have the guards setup the woodshop."

"If you had a picture of your granddaughter, it would help me get the sizing correct."

The warden pulled a picture out of his wallet. "This is her just last month at a piano recital. She was wearing her favorite red dress."

The warden lingered on the picture for a minute before passing it Lucas. "Will you need any help?"

"I would rather complete this project on my own, boss. For a piece this complex, it would help if I could stay in the woodshop overnight. I would want to stain each piece individually as they are finished, and I could rest in between staining sessions. If I can borrow a pen and some paper I can write down the items I will need."

The warden handed Lucas a pen and note pad. He then called for Simon and gave him instructions to send someone out to open the woodshop. He also told the guard to make sure someone brought in a bunk and some bedding and to make sure that Lucas had all the food and drinks he wanted over the weekend. He pulled a hundred-dollar bill out of his wallet and told the guard to add it to Lucas' commissary account.

"This is everything I need boss." Lucas handed him the list.

"The brass fittings, hinges, and bars are a little hard to find, so I wrote down my son's phone number. He should have all these items in stock, along with some good quality slabs of oak. His workshop is only an hour's drive from here, and they have a driver that can deliver everything."

"I really appreciate this Lucas. I will make sure you have everything as soon as possible today. Is there anything else you need?"

"No, boss. That should be everything. I should get to the woodshop and start making preparations."

The warden motioned for Simon to walk over. "Take Mister Fosterman to the woodshop, and make sure he has everything he needs to get started."

Peace and Quiet

It had been nearly forty hours and Lucas had made great progress. He had already completed all the woodwork on the coffin. Since he had stained each piece of wood individually before fastening, the coffin looked mostly finished before he even started carving.

He was frustrated by how long it took to carve the intricate lines of flowers. Only a few years ago, he could have moved twice as fast. But he was older now and sorely out of practice with doing custom work. Even though the work had taken longer than expected, he was still happy with the end results. The top of the coffin was surrounded with a perimeter of flowers. Another line of flowers followed the circumference of the coffin just above the brass handles.

Lucas applied one final coat of thick, shiny lacquer to the piece and turned on the fan to help it dry. He then focused his attention on the red fabric that would be used to line the coffin. He cut strips of fabric and glued it to the filler material.

Another three hours passed before the varnish was dry

enough to start lining the coffin. He worked slowly, stitching in the deep red fabric. He made sure to keep everything tight and even as he worked. It was nearly complete when the warden walked into the woodshop.

"Good evening, Mister Fosterman."

"Good evening, boss." Lucas stood up and stepped back to allow the warden to move in for a closer look. "I am getting close. I just need another hour to finish the liner and a couple more hours to complete the finish work."

"It looks amazing. It is perfect for our Jody," said the warden as he inspected the coffin. He slowly walked all the way around the four-foot box, checking out every inch. He was very impressed with the quality of the work, the smooth rich finish, and the exquisite carvings.

He lifted the lid to look inside. "She would love the red fabric, and it is so soft."

He took a closer look at the foot of the coffin and furrowed his brow. "What is the small box at the end there?"

"I thought she might want to take her little puppy with her," said Lucas. "But I can leave that out if you had other plans."

The warden was stunned by the thought. He hadn't even considered burying the two together. He had remained composed, almost business like, to this point. But the thought of burying his granddaughter with her little puppy was more than the man could bear. He slumped down on a stool and buried his head in his hands.

Lucas wasn't sure what to do. He wanted to console the man, but he knew better than to touch the warden. No matter how unusual a situation this was, he was still a prisoner, and prisoners never touched the warden.

Thankfully, lead guard Jerry walked in a few seconds later carrying a plate of food and a bottle of root beer. He handed the tray to Lucas and motioned for him to move to the other side of the table.

The guard walked over to the warden. "It is a beautiful coffin, Rex," said the guard putting his hand on his back. It was the first time Lucas had ever heard anyone use the warden's first name. "Why don't we get you home to your family, and I will take it to the funeral home when Lucas is finished with it later today."

The warden nodded and stood up. He grabbed a clean rag from the table, wiped his eyes, and blew his nose. The two men started walking out of the shop, but the warden stopped and walked over to Lucas.

"Thank you, sir. It is simply perfect. I wouldn't change a thing." To the surprise of everyone, the warden reached and shook Lucas' hand. "Someday, I will find a way to repay you for this. I don't know how and I don't know when, but I will think of something."

With that the two men left the woodshop. Lucas was left alone in the large open area. He looked down at his plate, which was filled with much more food than he needed. He had two hamburgers, an extra-large portion of fries, and three brownies.

He took his time eating, reviewing everything that had happened over the past two days. He couldn't believe how immune he had been to the sorrow of the situation. The act of building a coffin for a man's young granddaughter should have flooded his emotions. He felt sorry for the warden, but that sorrow had not affected Lucas the way he thought it would.

He reasoned that he had lived with Katie's death for so long now that it had become a part of him. He thought about her every day, so a new reminder did little to impact his constant level of sorrow.

The only thing that did add a new degree of sadness was the idea of the little puppy also dying in the crash. Lucas had always been fond of animals, and he would never forget the first time he lost a dog. He still missed his old friend Pedro.

Avenging Mighty Pedro

"Men regard it as their right to return evil for evil and, if they cannot, feel they have lost their liberty."

— *Aristotle*

Summer 1954

The Mighty Pedro

In every neighborhood there is a guardian of sorts. One who surveys the land and ensures his presence is felt at every corner, at every happenstance. The grand rooster, the big steer. In this neighborhood that position was held by Pedro, Lucas Fosterman's miniature Chihuahua.

Pedro stood a stout nine inches high and weighed an easy eight pounds. He was covered head to paw in short, jet-black fur, his build similar to a seasoned fighting pit bull. He had a fierce disposition toward anyone or anything that wondered into the area without proper identification.

Pedro could usually be found strutting from one end of the block and back again, keeping the peace, enforcing justice. There was nothing that happened on Pear Street that escaped the attention of the mighty Chihuahua. Stray dogs and cats were run off within seconds. Strangers were accosted immediately. Even approaching vehicles were not allowed safe passage.

Lucas never tired of watching Pedro harass dogs ten times his size. His high-pitched yipping and shear confidence disheartened the bravest of opponents. He was the embodiment of machismo.

The only other dog allowed safe passage on the block was his friend Matt's black Labrador retriever, Misty. Misty was a fluffy sixty-pound ball of playfulness and Pedro had been smitten with her for quite some time.

Misty was his girl. And no one messes with Pedro's girl.

However, in the summer of 1954 this presented a problem for the Chihuahua. Misty had recently gone into heat, and suitors were arriving in droves. The miniature guard had run himself ragged beating back any would-be perverts brave enough to enter his domain.

Lucas, Matt, and their friend Jack sat on Lucas' front porch for most of the day. It was a slow sunny Wednesday afternoon, and they still hadn't thought up anything better to do. Too hot to play football. Too lazy to walk to the fishing hole. Besides, the Pedro show was entertainment enough.

Taking a break from guard duty, Pedro decided it was time to check in on Misty and see if he could get a little action. Misty was up for a romp, but the mathematical differences of the pair made the situation a lost cause. Even standing on two legs, Pedro barely reached the top of Misty's hindquarters. This setback did little to thwart the mighty Pedro. His walnut-size brain worked up an ingenious plan and he immediately set into action.

The plan seemed simple: Pedro stood on the fourth step of the porch, while Misty positioned her backside to him. He jumped into position and went to town humping away furiously. The only problem was that Misty's backside was sloped in such a way that the little guy couldn't get a decent grip. He flew through the air, scrambled for position, and got in four or five good pumps before sliding off his prize.

The scene was hilarious and the boys couldn't contain themselves. Howling with laughter, they watched as Pedro shot the one-foot gap between the stairs and his target. Matt laughed so hard he couldn't breathe, and Jack fell off the porch grabbing his gut. They cackled at the show a while longer before Lucas' mom peeked out the screen door to see what the commotion was all about.

"Pedro, you stop that right now!" she yelled, trying to contain her own giggles. "You boys ought to be ashamed of yourselves watching that kind of stuff. What if he actually gets her pregnant?"

This caused the boys to laugh even harder. The thought of a Lab/Chihuahua mix puppy was more than the mind could process. Lucas' mom threw up her hands and returned to the house, still stifling her giggles.

The comedy act continued for another half hour before Pedro

was called back to duty by an approaching vehicle.

A banana-yellow Cadillac slowly rounded the corner. It was an early 30's model and a boat of a car. It sported a rusty tailpipe that spewed clouds of gray smoke. Pedro was beside himself with anger; barking, whining and jumping wildly about.

The car settled itself directly across the street from Lucas' house and out stepped the vilest woman to ever walk God's green Earth – The Bat.

The Bat was an eighty-something woman who walked squarely upright, but still carried a cane. No one had ever seen her limp. The cane was simply her weapon of choice. She had typical blue-gray old lady hair and was wearing a frumpy, long-sleeve, puke-green dress. Her face was covered chin to brow in a horrible scowl. Cruella Deville's fat evil twin.

A plume of cigarette smoke followed her out of the car, and she mumbled something across the roof. The passenger was a kindly, but sad looking man. He was hunched over from an arthritic back and was carrying a paper sack containing what looked to be a bottle of whiskey. Medicine for the pain. He simply ignored whatever was said and indifferently walked toward the house.

The Bat shook her head in disgust and turned her attention to the irate animal nipping at her heels. She let out a stream of curses and made a feeble attempt at kicking the dog. This did little to derail his persistence. She poked out her cane with the precision of Black Beard wielding a cutlass. It eventually clipped Pedro on his front leg causing him to let out a quick yelp. Changing tactics, the Chihuahua started running around the old woman as fast as his stubby legs would carry him. The new strategy appeared to be working, as Pedro darted in and out scoring nip after nip.

The Bat, red faced and huffing, turned to scream at Lucas. "You better get this damned dog away from me before I kill the little rat bastard! I just bought a new box of twenty-two shells with his name on them!"

"You better leave my dog alone, you senile old witch! I'll kick your ass if you touch him!" Lucas hollered back.

"You just try it you little punk! Damn kids and their untrained bastard animals!"

The Bat continued her cursing, kicking, and poking as she unloaded her groceries and made her way to the front door. Pedro kept at her all the while, but stopped abruptly at the bottom of the stairs. Even the bravest of warriors hesitate to attack the enemy in their headquarters. This move proved wise, as The Bat returned to battle, broom in hand. She took a few swipes at the elusive target as Pedro made a hasty retreat.

Down, but not defeated, the little general protected his dignity by dropping a couple of tootsie-roll size turds on The Bat's lawn. This sent the old woman into hysterics. She launched off the porch with the speed and grace of an NFL running back. The squatting Chihuahua barely escaped the bristles of the broom, as he sped off toward home. The old woman pumped her fist in the air. "I'll get you. I swear!"

Lucas, Matt, and Jack howled with laughter. Jack fell off the porch again. The old woman shot them another wicked scowl and stomped into the house.

Pedro, having finished his duties, returned to his mating circus.

On with the show.

The Audacious Event

For the next few days The Bat paced her front deck like a Nazi general. This worried Lucas, mainly because the wretch wasn't holding her usual arsenal of a cane or broom. In fact, the only thing she carried was one of the disgusting mini-stogies she smoked constantly.

Strange activity indeed.

There was a disquieting demeanor about her, almost a calm resolve. She had even stopped her usual barrage of insults as neighbors passed in front of her house. She simply marched back and forth from sun up to sun down.

The old man seemed unaffected by the strange behavior. He sat silently in his oversized wooden chair, sipping from his brown paper bag. Occasionally whittling on a branch.

Even brave Pedro appeared nervous over the change in enemy activity. He took wide routes around The Bat's yard, keeping a wary eye trained on her at all times. Sometimes he sat on the edge of the blue hair's property line and stared at her for long periods. This caused The Bat to pause her marching and stare back at the small dog.

This strangeness continued until Sunday afternoon. The boys sat in Lucas' room sneaking peeks at his dad's pinup collection. Jack was showing Matt a picture of a particularly busty redhead when they heard the loud crack of a rifle shot. This was immediately followed by a short yelp, then silence.

They all looked up at each other with knowing glances, too shocked to move. A tear started to well up in Lucas' eye, and they all rushed to the front door.

The Bat was standing in her front doorway holding a .22 rifle. She gave the boys an evil smirk and closed the door behind her.

That was when Lucas saw him... Pedro lying in The Bat's yard, barely a foot from the sidewalk. He was curled up into a ball and looked almost peaceful. The only giveaway was a well of dark red blood pooling at the base of his neck.

Lucas was beside himself with grief and anger. Jack and Matt had to restrain him from charging the crazy women's house.

They stood dumbfounded in the street for what felt like an hour. Lucas was manic. He switched from fits of rage to complete sobbing. He loved that damn dog.

Jack focused his attention on trying to calm Lucas down, while Matt started to seethe with anger. They couldn't believe the pure cold-heartedness of the act. How could anyone simply kill an innocent animal? And right in front of the whole neighborhood? Retribution must be had.

Mighty Pedro had fallen. The Bat must suffer.

The Burial and the Plan

The burial was short and somber. The boys fit together a passable cross and placed it at the head of the small grave. Misty plopped down next to the mound and started to whimper. The site of the scorned lover was too much for Lucas to bear.

He quickly finished sobbing and started focusing on anger and revenge.

The boys sat for hours thinking of various plans to strike at the heart of the enemy, working through several scenarios.

Lucas was convinced that they should burn down her house. Jack surmised that this would just give the wretch reason to report them to the proper authorities. Arson would surely result in an investigation and eventually incarceration. Too risky.

Matt suggested a string of prank calls and other irritating devises. Simply not solid enough retribution.

Lucas sat quietly for a while, when suddenly it hit him. It was ingenious, flawless. Simply wonderful. Until now, the irony of the situation had escaped him. The Bat had a cat.

The Bat hated all forms of life trespassing on her property, but she did nothing to keep her frisky feline from roaming the neighborhood. On most afternoons, the fluffy hairball could be seen sunning on Matt's propane tank in his back yard.

They discussed a few choice details and sprang into action. Supplies had to be gathered: a gunnysack, clippers, and a pail of red paint.

Later that afternoon they gathered on Lucas' back porch spying on the ugly tabby lounging peacefully on the tank. They sat in silence waiting for the perfect moment to strike.

Finally, luck gave them a break. The Bat's shrill voice could be heard as she headed out her front door. "Get a move on, you lazy buzzard!" She shouted at her husband. He simply looked at his feet and continued moving at his usual slow pace.

The loathsome woman marched pointedly to her car and

ripped open the driver-side door. She searched the area for someone to sneer at. Finding no victims, she plopped into the seat and cranked the banana mobile to a smog-producing start. The old man crawled into the metal carriage showing complete ambivalence toward the squawking wretch next to him.

The car sputtered away. The boys looked at each other knowingly.

Time for action.

Lucas, gunnysack in hand, circled behind the propane tank. Jack and Matt crept forward to block any avenues of escape. The fat fur ball continued to lie in purring bliss. Lucas moved in closer with the sack and quickly slapped it over the animal. An easy capture. The cat didn't even startle until it was securely contained in the bag.

The hostage was taken.

The once docile feline sounded more like a mountain lion as it protested its new predicament. The boys ran full throttle, bag in tow, for the small shed at the corner of Lucas' house. They rushed in and pulled the door shut. Matt switched on the bare light bulb.

Surveying the faces, Lucas looked positively intent. A boy of pure purpose. Jack looked a bit bewildered, but a slight smirk gave away a menacing quality that was sure to grow with time. Matt looked pale. He was not looking forward to removing the wild creature from the bag for the next phase of the plan.

Luckily, Lucas was willing to take one for the team. He jabbed a hand into the bag and haphazardly grabbed for the crazed animal. After several yelps of pain from both boy and animal, his arm appeared... cat in hand. His limb showed dozens of scratch marks and small beads of blood started to pop up in spots. No one said revenge would be easy.

Lucas had the beast by the neck and was having trouble keeping it steady. Jack helped by grabbing the front and rear legs and Matt shouted for Lucas to grab the clippers.

Lucas pulled out the clippers and stabbed the plug into an old electrical socket, which gave him quite a jolt. The powers that be did not approve.

Bolstered by the pain, Lucas clicked the on button and aimed the clippers at the victim.

The cat, lying face down, began to spasm wildly as Lucas shaved a clean patch up its back. He stepped back, admiring his work before leading the shears back into action. The clippers made quick work of the feline's backside. Three minutes and a dozen scratches later only a few specks of fur could be found on the quivering animal's back. Lucas stared at the naked beast feeling a twinge of guilt for stripping it of its natural clothing.

"Snap out of it and grab the paint!" yelled Matt.

Lucas shuffled around on the shelf until he found the brush and jabbed it into the bucket of paint. Candy apple red. A wonderful color.

Matt snatched the brush away from Lucas, launching large drops of red paint all around the shack. He sized up the target and began brushing deliberate diagonal stripes across the creatures back and belly.

He quickly recharged the brush, knocking over the paint bucket in the process. He ended by shellacking the tail with two coats of glossy redness.

"Stand back! I'm going to let her go!" yelled Lucas.

"Oh Crap!" Yelped Jack as he jumped backwards, slamming into wall.

Matt grabbed a trashcan lid to use as a shield and began wielding the paint brush like a knight of old.

Beware the red dragon.

Lucas still had a grip on the squirming red monster's neck and hips. He let it fly with a snap of his wrists. Landing on its feet, the shocked cat crouched in a defensive postured taking in its surroundings and hissing wildly.

Jack, seeing that the beast was lying directly in his path, began to inch to his left. He bumped into the edge of a table. Cans and tools clattered to the ground. Then all hell broke loose.

A whir of tan and red flashes surrounded the room. High, low, left, right, in every conceivable direction. Matt cowered in the corner, holding up his shield praying to Odin for help. Jack hopped around in a crazed frenzy, squealing wildly and desperately trying to avoid the menace. In his efforts to avoid contact with the beast, Jack slammed his shoulder into an old saw blade suffering a two-inch jagged gash on us upper bicep. Lucas picked up the gunnysack and swung it in self-defense. He tripped backward, landing hard on his bottom and smacking his head into the back wall.

The commotion broke suddenly. The angry feline was now perched on a high shelf, hissing. The hissing was both maddening and terrifying. Who knew a six-pound creature could strike such fear? But this was no ordinary animal. Quick analysis of the mad beast showed that Lucas had missed several tufts of fur in his shaving. This mixed with the sharp red stripes across its face and body made it look like a battle-worn Celtic warrior.

Seizing the momentary calm, Lucas rushed to the door and threw it open. The hostage wasted no time bolting to freedom. In his haste to avoid the red dragon Lucas fell sideways, twisting his ankle before falling hard to the ground and bruising his arm. With the smoke clear, the three boys looked at each other, short of breath, sweaty, fur-covered, and beaten.

Time to tend to the wounded.

Victory

For the next twelve hours, there was no sign of the red goblin. The anticipation was relentless. Was it dead? Hiding? Had The Bat found her defiled pet and decided to lie in wait to retaliate? The possibilities were endless.

Jack paced the floor ranting about the punishment that was sure to come. Lucas found delight in retelling the event over and over. Matt stayed glued to the window keeping a close watch on the ominous door across the way. There hadn't been a sign of life for what seemed like an eternity.

Then she appeared. The decrepit old woman crept out her front door, cane in hand. Her face showed an even-larger scowl than usual. She glared at Lucas' bedroom window for a moment, which made Matt's heart jump. He dashed below the windowsill.

"What is it?" Squawked Jack, seeing his reaction.

"It's her, she's coming out."

"What's she doing?"

"Hell if I know. I think she might have seen me looking out the window."

"Holy crap," whispered Lucas as he ducked under the sill next to Matt.

Jack quickly joined them. They sat in silence fearing she may be able to hear even the faintest whispers. They were too scared to look out the window.

That's when it started. The yelling. "Agatha!" She crowed. "Agatha!"

Her voice was grating, damn near cartoonish. She screeched the name over and over walking from one end of the block to the other. She never used any of the usual catcalls like "Here kitty, kitty" or "Here girl." She just said the cat's name over and over. "Agatha!… Agatha!… Agatha!… Agatha!… Agatha!"

They stayed cooped up in Lucas's room for two hours as she continued her search. They tried to entertain themselves with cards and comic books, but the incessant calls of "Agatha!" keep ringing in their ears.

Finally, the madness stopped with the slamming of a screen door. Peace at last. They jumped to the window. The street was empty. Not a person in sight. No cars. No dogs. No Cats… Wait. There it was. In the far corner of the block, a glint of red could be seen strolling up the far end of the street.

"Look. At the end of the block!" Jack pointed down the street.

"That's one ugly tabby," Matt critiqued. "Did it look that bad in the shed? I knew we did a good job, but damn."

"Where's it headed?" Asked Jack, squinting due to his

atrocious eyesight. "I can't see it."

"Holy crap, it's going in the house. Hide."

Back under the windowsill none of them could breathe. The oxygen had been removed from the room. What's next? Beatings, prison, death?

Hell's a comin' boys.

The reaction was immediate. An awful sound rang out of The Bat's house. They could hear yelling. Incomplete sentences. Only bits of curse words and phrases. There were also allusions to disembowelment and other bodily harm.

Then the loud bang of a screen door made the boys jump and their eyes widen. "You'll pay for this, you bastards! I know you can hear me! You're going to be put away for life! You're going to be butt raped by giant Puerto Rican gangsters in prison! Rat bastards!"

Another sound of a slamming screen door rang out and more incoherent curses. The tension was still high, but Matt could no longer stifle his laughter. As soon as he started laughing, Lucas joined in, then Jack. They laughed for a good three minutes. Doom was coming. Prison, beatings, pain, the whole lot. But for the moment they were victorious kings.

Vengeance had been extracted.

Officer Bradley

About an hour later a police car pulled up to The Bat's house. It was a black and white 1950 Chevy Bel-Air with a single round red light on the roof.

Matt, Jack, and Lucas looked to each other with relief in their hearts. The car belonged to Officer Bradley. A nice man and the father of their friend Henry.

They watched as Officer Bradley hiked up his belt and sauntered up to the screen door. He took a quick glance around. Seeing the boys peeking through the window, he gave them a friendly nod. He shook his head then knocked on the screen door.

A second later he walked in The Bat's house to sounds of a renewed cursing frenzy. Lucas dashed into his closet in search of some unknown item. Matt and Jack began concocting a few passable alibis and settled on being in the bedroom all afternoon playing cards during the "alleged" kidnapping and animal defiling.

Clothes flew out of the closet as Jack related the alibi to Lucas. He grunted his approval and found what he has been looking for in the form of a blue-toned flannel shirt to cover his myriad of scratches. He slipped it on and the boys headed outside to sit on the porch. Best to face the matter head on.

They arranged themselves in nonchalant positions as they awaited the inquisition. Finally, Officer Bradley backed out of the doorway, nodding all the while. You could tell he was trying to calm the seething woman. "I'll look into it." His tone was soothing as he walked away.

"You better. Those kids better be behind bars by dawn. Filthy cretins."

The patient officer headed down the stairs, hiked up his belt again, and walked toward the three lounging, cool cats sitting easily on the porch.

"Good afternoon boys. How are things?"

"Good for us Mister Bradley. How's Henry? Still at summer camp?" Matt asked.

"He's having a good time. Be back next Monday."

"What brings you to our side of town?" blurted Jack, nerves giving him away.

"Well, the neighbor's cat seems to have been vandalized in a very deliberate way."

"That's odd," Matt said. "Just the other day Lucas' Chihuahua turned up dead with a gunshot wound to the neck. Must be some sort of epidemic."

"Yeah. The neighbor lady said she shot a dog trespassing on her property just the other day. Said it attacked her in her yard and bit a hole in her shoe. Claims it chased her onto her porch where she had a rifle sitting and shot it in self-defense."

"That's a damn lie!" Screamed Lucas. "She hunted Pedro down like a wild animal. He never did anything to her. She's a mean old coot who hates everyone and everything."

Realizing he had severely compromised their position, Lucas sank back onto the porch staring at his feet. Damn his feeble emotions.

Officer Bradley acted taken aback by the outburst. "Now boys you didn't have anything to do with that cat did you?"

"W-we were sitting at home p-playing c-cards all d-d-day," Jack stammered.

One look at Officer Bradley's face showed that he wasn't buying the alibi. Maybe it was the way Matt's face turned bright red every time he looked at him. Maybe it was the sudden stutter Jack had developed. Or maybe it was the fact that Lucas was wearing a long sleeve flannel shirt in 100-degree temperature in an attempt to cover up the scratches on his arms. In any case, the jig was up.

"Aw crap, we did it," Lucas blurted out. "We can't lie to you Mister Bradley. The Old Bat shot my dog, and we had to retaliate. That mean old lady has been bullying us for years, and this time she just went too far."

"Shut up, they're going to lock us up and throw away the key!" Jack muttered.

Silence loomed as the boys looked at each other and back to the suddenly ominous looking Officer Bradley.

A wave of emotions washed over them as they waited for the sentencing. What was it going be? Two, three, maybe four years in the hoosegow. What was the going rate for cat mutilation these days? Surely, they would go easy on Jack. He was only twelve for goodness sake. But Matt and Lucas were fourteen. Practically grown men. They would probably stick them in with the general population, with the rapists, murderers, and other pet defilers.

Lucas' stomach began to lurch. He felt a strange sickness

coming on. Then something odd happened.

Officer Bradley began a hearty laugh and patted Lucas on the head, which caused his shaky knees to wobble and he slumped back on the porch.

"Boys. I probably should be mad at you, but I'll be damned if I wouldn't have done something just as stupid when I was younger. That old bird is a tough nut."

A wave of relief washed over the boys. Maybe prison wasn't in their future after all. Could they dare hope to get off scot-free?

"Still, I'll have to tell your parents and some sort of punishment will have to be arranged. Plus, there will be the matter of a vet bill."

Oh crap! Until now none of the boys had considered their parents. They were so certain they would be hauled away without trial that the thought of involving their parents had escaped them. Being locked away for a year or two didn't sound too bad all of a sudden.

Jack began sobbing immediately. His father was a retired Army drill instructor. A mountain of a man who delivered punishment with giant meaty paws.

Matt didn't look as worried. His father had gone to prison when he was five, and his mother was not much on tough punishments. He was more worried about disappointing her than anything.

As for Lucas, he was also screwed. His mother would come unglued, and he could already envision his father taking off his belt.

Revenge is a bitter pill.

Judgment Day

As luck would have it, Officer Bradley was able to catch Lucas' parents returning from the grocery store with Matt's mom in tow. He related the boys' transgressions to the attentive jurors. Sentencing was handed out immediately. Matt's red-faced mother graciously recruited Lucas' father to hand out the beatings for both boys.

Officer Bradley left the dirty work to Lucas' dad and headed off to speak with Jack's father.

On with the beatings. Lucas was up first.

Alone, it would not have been nearly as bad, but with an audience waiting in line behind the closed bedroom door it turned into pure hell. Bare bottom, belt swinging, long lecture on the improprieties of defiling innocent animals, more belt swinging, more lecturing, and a hug for humanity.

Lucas walked out of the bathroom still sniffling, rubbing his throbbing hindquarters. He caught a glimpse of a pale-faced Matt as he passed. It was hard to make eye contact with a condemned man.

Lucas stood at the bathroom sink straining to hear sounds from the bathroom. It was quiet for a few minutes. Then five loud snaps. A few yelps. A scream and a sustained cry. The deed was done in less than three minutes. The boy got off easy.

Still, Lucas couldn't keep from giggling at the thought of Matt whining like a baby. What is it that made boys laugh in moments like this? He supposed it was the same reason grown men still find it funny to see other men get kicked in the groin. Foul beasts.

Lucas rinsed his face in the sink and took a long look at himself in the mirror. He was a very skinny kid, but tall for his age. His hair had turned a light brown in the past couple of years instead of the bright blonde "tow head" he had suffered with throughout his grade school days. His skin was overly pale, even for a Midwestern white boy. At the moment, his face looked sickly and opaque with tear tracks running down under both eyes.

He washed his face again and conducted a thorough inspection to ensure there were no signs of tears or other weakness. The authorities may have convicted him, but he was still convinced his actions were justified.

The Chain Gang

The next day Matt and Lucas found themselves dressed in gray coveralls picking up trash on the side of Highway 50. Hot, sweaty, thirsty, pissed off, and walking bowlegged from still sore back sides.

It had only been thirty minutes and Matt was already complaining.

"Are you kidding me? Thirty-nine and a half more hours of this crap. I'll go mad. And why do we have to wear these stupid outfits?"

"All in the name of rehabilitation." Lucas fumed.

"Rehabilitation my ass. Where's the rehabilitation for that old witch. She should be out here with us for all the grief she's caused. I'll tell you one thing. This ain't over. I'm going to make her pay. First your dog, then my ass, now we're stuck out here doing this humiliating crap."

"Well, we've got plenty of time to work out some proper payback."

Matt nodded in agreement and looked up. A truck was speeding up the hill. Loud, rusty, red, and spewing smog. It rumbled to a stop and out plopped Jack, dressed in his chain gang uniform.

"Have fun boys!" Grumbled Jack's dad as he rolled away.

One look showed that Jack had taken the brunt of their blundering. No friendly greetings. Just a slight nod hello and a slow waddle to his trash picking tools. He winced as he bent down to pick up a green garbage bag and poking stick.

"Jesus Jack, are you okay?" Matt asked walking up to him. "Where did you get it?"

Jack didn't say a word. He just opened the side of his coveralls showing a large bruise stretching from the top of his hip to middle of his thigh. "The other side looks the same," he explained.

"That's messed up. What's your old man trying to prove?" snorted Matt.

"Forget about it," Jack said, buttoning himself back up. "Let's just figure out a way to pay that wicked witch back."

Matt and Lucas looked at each other in amazement. After a beating like that, how could anyone be so willing to jump right back into the fire? Balls of steel.

Seeing their reactions, Jack shook his head and started stabbing his poker into wads of trash. "I'm not going to take this crap lying down. We didn't start this war, but we're damn sure going to win it."

Bolstered by Jack's determination, the boys launched into their roadside cleaning with renewed vigor.

Five days later, sunburned, blisters on their feet, and dog tired, they completed their community service. The hot sun had kept them from developing a truly great retaliation plan, so they settled on a traditional prank to tide them over. A bag of manure, a can of gas, and a lighter would equal one pissed off old bat.

Run Fool Run

***

In the fall of 1912 Winchester Firearms introduced the Model 12 Pump Shotgun. The thirty-inch cobalt blue barrel, checkered wood pump handle, and molded stock made it an attractive and utilitarian weapon. Depending on the setup, the shotgun could hold up to six 20-gauge shells, which could be filled with a variety of loads. To this day, all three boys can still remember the first time they looked upon that magnificent weapon.

***

The boys waited until midnight before heading to Lucas' shed to make their preparations. The inside of the wooden shack still showed the leftovers of their last criminal act. Fur lined the floor and paint fumes still lingered.

Matt pulled out a large paper bag and started filling it with large clumps of cow dung that his mother had lying in a mound to fertilize her roses. He then scoured the lawn for other pieces of animal feces to add to the collection. Rabbit, cat, squirrel, anything smelly, and flammable. He even made sure to add a couple of Pedro's miniature turds to the mix out of respect for the dead.

Once the bag was about half full, he rolled down the top and doused it with gasoline.

The prank was set.

The trick was simple. The boys would sneak onto The Bat's front porch, set the bag down, light it, ring the doorbell, and run like hell. The Old Bat would see the flaming bag and stomp it out, getting dung all over her foot. Simple, immature, but flawless.

Quick deliberation and a losing round of rock, paper, scissors volunteered Lucas to be the front man. Jack and Matt agreed to back him up at the top of the stairs.

Lucas gripped the bag in his right hand, lighter in the left as they made their way around the side of the enemy camp. The neighborhood seemed darker than usual that night. Better for stealth.

Jack stumbled over a fallen tree branch causing a snapping noise. Matt warned him to be quiet in a much too loud voice. Lucas told them both to shut up as they approached the first step.

Lucas looked around cautiously, looking for signs of life. No guards on duty.

The screen door had been left open, but a big wooden main door sheltered them from view. A quick glance in the window showed that the TV was still on. There was white fuzz showing on the screen. The old man was snoring in his recliner. No sign of the evil one.

Lucas took a breath. He looked back at his reinforcements,

which had just cleared the last step and were keeping close watch on the windows.

The crinkling bag plopped down in front of the door. Lucas began feeble attempts at clicking the lighter. His thumb, blistered from wielding the trash poker, had trouble spinning the flint wheel. After three tries he switched hands. Click. Click. Bastard device. Click. Click. Sweet holy crap, there was fire. The blue flame mesmerized him for a moment when suddenly the sound of a rattling doorknob shook him from his stupor.

Unleash the Kraken. Every man for himself.

In a flash, the front door swung open. The ominous old cow stood dressed in a thin blue cotton robe with her hair in a net. She scowled at the lot of them. Her scowl slowly turned to an evil grin as she pulled out Winchester's Model 12 from behind the wall, pumped it once for effect, and raised it to her shoulder.

Until now they had been frozen in terror. The sight of the shotgun awakened a survival reflex, and Lucas was the first to fly into action.

"Run like hell!" he shouted while spinning and launching off the top step of the porch. A loud bang rang in his ears and he felt a sharp pain slam into his upper thigh, just below his left butt cheek. There was also a sound similar to breaking glass. Must be the sound of death he reasoned.

He hit the ground stumbling wildly, but was still able to run forward.

A pumping sound, then a second blast rang. "Aw God," Jack screamed.

Lucas looked back to see Jack sprawled out on the top of the steps, scrambling furiously to get to his feet. His ass and leg were covered in a chalky white powder.

A third pump. Matt had made it to the bottom of the stairs and was rushing away. Run, boy, run. But The Bat was on him. A third blast struck him square in the ass and made him lurch forward. He winced and stumbled, but managed to keep moving.

Jack finally made it to his feet and dashed off the stairs. He was helped along by a fourth blast that hit his thigh and caused him to land awkwardly. He tried to make it to his feet, but his ankle slid sideways and he was on the ground again, this time screaming and grabbing his leg. Lucas and Matt rushed back for him, watching as the gunslinger slammed the door closed.

Still scrambling, the boys reached Jack and carried him away from the scene. They were immediately greeted at the front porch of Lucas' house by his dad, mom, and grandma. "What the hell is going on out here?" Yelled Lucas' dad. "What happened to you boys?"

"The old bag shot us. She got Jack twice." Lucas started to tear up. Until now, he had forgotten about his wounded leg. With the adrenaline subsiding, the pain started to flood in.

"Am I going to die?" Matt pleaded.

Lucas' dad walked up to Matt, spun him around and inspected the wound. "It's just rock salt. You'll live. But if you think it hurts now, wait 'til you start picking that crap out of your ass."

"I think Jack's got a broken foot," offered Matt. "And he got shot twice, point blank."

Lucas' dad walked behind Jack for closer inspection. The look on his face let everyone know Jack had gotten the worst of it again. He's one unlucky bastard.

Lucas stood there sniffling, going over the events in his head. The images were staggering. The Bat had gotten off four shots and every one of them had hit their mark. She had wielded that shotgun with military precision and pumped out shots without mercy.

"What did you boys do?" asked Lucas' dad, trying to hide a smile. "I'm sure that old lady didn't start shooting at you without provocation."

"We just put a bag on her doorstep. That's all."

"A bag?" Lucas' mom sounded confused. "A bag of what?"

"The old flaming bag of crap routine? That's a little juvenile even for you boys," explained Lucas' dad, no longer trying to hide his smile. He was enjoying this. Then suddenly his expression changed to a look of panic. "Mom!"

The boys followed his gaze until they saw that Lucas' grandma had walked across the street and was climbing The Bat's porch steps. "Mom!"

Grandma Fosterman was a rather large woman, roughly 280 pounds and not all blubber. Her bulk was the product of seventy years of manual labor, hearty portions of corn-fed beef, and self-gardened vegetables, all melded with a dose of old fashioned grit. She was not a tea and crumpets lady, with a white couch and pretty knick-knacks. She was the kind of lady that changed her own oil, mowed her own lawn, and chopped her own wood. She was kind to everyone… as long as they didn't mess with her family.

"Mom!" Yelled Lucas' dad a little more forcefully. But he was too late. Grandma Fosterman was already at the door, beating on it rather rudely.

"MOM!"

The door opened and out walked The Bat, still clutching her shotgun. "What's the meaning of this?" She roared.

Not being a woman of many words, Grandma Fosterman answered her with a magnificent right cross directly between the eyes.

The Bat fell like a sack of potatoes. A perfect knockout.

No grandson had ever felt so proud. God bless grandmothers everywhere.

The Pain, The Glory

Lucas laid across the side of his bed looking like a broken-down shotgun. His bare bottom pointed up, shining under the hot light of a lamp positioned a couple feet away. His mom concentrated intently as she plucked BB sized chunks of white salt from his left butt cheek. She had been plucking for fifteen minutes now, and he still yelped every time a new chunk was removed. The entire left side of his body felt like it was on fire.

"Aww! Wait, wait! Awww! How many more are there?" He wailed.

"If you would stop squirming around it would make this go a lot faster. Hold still."

Five more plucks. Five more screams.

"There, I think I got it all. Now, go get in the shower and wash it off," she said helping him get up. "And tell Matt to get in here."

He passed by Matt stifling his sniffles. No need to look like a wimp.

"Your turn," he said, not making eye contact.

He had thought the plucking was unbearable, but that pain was nothing compared to what he felt as soon as the warm water hit the wounded area. Luckily, he had stuck a wash cloth in his mouth to prevent Matt from hearing his squealing. The pain was an excruciating mix of burning and stabbing sensations. His leg shook uncontrollably, but he could see the white salt disappearing and blood start to wash away. After the shock wore off, the water started to have a soothing effect, and he was able to calm his spasms. Inspecting the wound, he saw that the damage wasn't nearly as bad as the pain would suggest.

A few bandages later and Lucas and Matt were fit for duty. They sat impatiently at the table as Lucas' mom talked to Jack's mother on the phone.

"I see. It is broken, then. My goodness, twenty-five stitches. That's horrible. Tetanus shot? That's a good idea. Yes, girls would have been easier. No, I think I know who to blame for this one. Yes, please call us when you get home. Bye now." Throughout the conversation, Lucas' mom continued to shoot her son looks of disappointment.

"Well. Jack's got a broken leg and had to get twenty-five stitches on his right side. I hope you boys are happy with yourselves," she said pouring on the guilt. "And who knows what's going to happen to your grandmother. Your dad is still down at the station trying to get her out."

Lucas and Matt stared into their cups of hot chocolate and plates of apple pie. Even after acts of despicable behavior mothers can't help but serve tasty treats to wounded warriors.

Once Lucas' mom departed the room, Matt looked up with a giant smile on his face. "Did you see that punch and the way that old hag fell like a sack of potatoes? That was the most beautiful thing I have ever seen."

"And did you see how crazy she got when Officer Bradley woke her up with the smelling salts?" Lucas said. "I thought she was going to have a heart attack running around all crazy and cursing like that."

Lucas had hated watching Officer Bradley take his grandma away, but at least he had the decency not to put her in handcuffs. Still, Grandma Fosterman's actions were noble and something the boys would cherish forever.

A sound at the door returned them to silence.

Lucas' dad walked in, shooting them a stern look. Lucas' mom met him in the kitchen and he sat at the table. "Well, Mom is back at home. She's just lucky she didn't have her medication on her, otherwise, they would've made her stay the night. She has to be back in tomorrow morning for a hearing."

"Oh my," Lucas' mom intoned. "I can't believe this."

"Matt, I talked to your mom. She'll be back in two days, and you're grounded. You're both grounded and don't ask for how long. Forever at this point. Spanking you obviously had no effect on your behavior. I'm sure those shotgun wounds have given you something to think about, but don't go thinking you're going to get off with just a grounding. You boys are going to work your butts to the bone. You have one hell of a debt to repay your grandma. I think four chords of wood should be enough to get her through the winter."

"FOUR CHORDS!" Lucas blurted, realizing the blunder right away.

"Make it five! And if she spends one more minute in jail because of you idiots, you'll be hauling wood, painting houses, mending fences, and doing every odd job I can think of for the entire summer!"

"Oh my," Lucas' mother whispered.

Oh my indeed.

Justice is Served with a Side of Guilt

Lucas and Matt sat in the living room staring at an unplugged TV. Too tired to talk. Every muscle they had ached after three full days of serving as lumber jacks.

Their parents were at the kitchen table relating their transgressions to Matt's mom, who had just returned from her trip. Matt looked ambivalent as he rubbed his sore right arm.

A knock sounded at the door, and Lucas reluctantly got up to answer it.

Jack was standing there. He was wearing shorts, leg in a cast, white bandages wrapped down both thighs. But strangely, he was grinning wildly as he pushed past Lucas in a rush.

"The Bat is dead," he said. "She's dead."

"Who? What?" Lucas said.

"The Old Bat. She kicked the bucket last night in her sleep. Officer Bradley is over there now with the coroner."

All three boys rushed to the door just in time to see Officer Bradley and some other official man carrying the old lady on a gurney, her body wrapped in a white sheet. They placed the gurney into a waiting hearse and it drove away.

Officer Bradley turned to the old man, who was sitting on the porch whittling on a piece of wood his head hanging low. The old man stood up and greeted Officer Bradley. He shook his head no, and turned to walk into the house.

Lucas' dad walked out to meet Officer Bradley in the street. The boys rushed up to them, but were pushed back as they talked.

"Coroner says Missus Lilly had a stroke," Officer Bradley nodded toward the departing hearse. "I guess she's had some sort of tumor in her brain for the last couple of years that made her a bit crazy. Mister Lilly is waiting for their daughter to come in from Chicago. He's going to live with them. He also said not to worry about the charges on your mom."

Missus Lilly? Lucas always thought her name was Garswartsch or Kremlin or Hagel or something cruel and German sounding. Not Missus Lilly. And she had a daughter. This didn't sit well either. She was someone's mother, probably someone's grandmother. Until now, she had been The Bat... A proper nemesis. Now she was human, and a sick one at that. Damn it all.

The next day, Lucas, Matt, and Jack sat on the porch looking across at Mister Lilly as he whittled away on his stick. None of them knew how to act or what to say, so they decided to just sit quietly.

After a while, a blue Ford sedan pulled up to the house. Out climbed a middle-aged woman. She was normal looking... medium build, short brown hair, black dress, somber eyes. Her husband came around to join her, giving her a hug. He was wearing a black suit. He was also normal looking. Two others joined them, a teenage boy and a younger girl. Obviously, their children. They walked up to the house and hugged Mister Lilly.

Matt looked over to see Lucas starting to tear up. He noticed him and looked away.

Lucas stood up and wiped his eyes. "Damn that dog," he muttered walking into the house.

Prison Life – Year Seven

"How can you hide from what never goes away?"

– Heraclitus

Happy Holidays

The holidays in prison were always a mixed bag. Many prisoners were excited to see their families during extended visitor's hours. The short-timers were hopeful about the year ahead and knowing that they would be home for the next holiday season. Even the guards were friendlier and more relaxed about free-time hours.

Other inmates shuffled around in a fog of depression, knowing that they would never get to spend another Christmas at home or kiss their wives at the stroke of midnight on New Year's Eve. Men with young children were the most melancholy. Their guilt and shame was palpable as they walked the halls of the penitentiary and especially during Christmas services.

But no matter how an inmate felt about the holidays, there was one thing that almost always brought a small spot of joy – the food. During the holidays, the quality, quantity, and variety of food was improved dramatically. Christmas Day was especially wonderful, but even the time between Christmas and New Year's Day offered a marked improvement in grub.

It was noon on Christmas Day, and Lucas was enjoying a fine feast. He had a plate full of food: a whole Cornish game hen, corn on the cob, roasted fingerling potatoes, and a slice of peach pie. He knew there was no way he could eat it all, but he was certainly going to eat that piece of pie.

As he dug into his meal, he thought back on his morning. His sons Mark and Paul had come to visit him during the eight to eleven o'clock visitation block. It was rare that both men could make it to visit on the same day, and he considered it a grand Christmas present. Before their arrival, he had made them promise that they would come during the morning block and only the morning block.

During the holidays, inmates were allowed up to six hours of visitation time, three in the morning and three in the afternoon, but Lucas did not want his family spending their entire Christmas day sitting in a prison visitation room.

The visit had been warm and positive. His sons were doing well at home and at work, his grandson was doing well in the Marines, and the rest of the family was happy and healthy.

Everything they talked about brought joy to his heart. He knew much of that was by design because his sons purposely avoided bringing negative news during the holidays. Still, he could tell that they were genuinely happy.

Lucas had finished half his game hen, all his corn and most of his potatoes, when Steve sat down at his table. Steve was a kind, round man in his mid-forties. He was serving the last bit of a four-year sentence for insurance fraud, and Lucas knew him from the small Christian support group they both attended.

"Hi Fosty. Isn't this meal wonderful?"

"It certainly is."

"Did you see your boys today?"

"I saw them this morning. They are both doing well. How about you? Did you see your wife and son?"

A flash of pain crossed Steve's face, but he still managed to keep smiling. "No, not today. I told them it would be best to stay at home. I get out in two months, and we are going to celebrate Christmas when I get home. I just couldn't bear to see them in this place during another holiday."

"That sounds nice Steve. They will be happy to have you back at home."

The two men sat for another fifteen minutes finishing their meals. Steve did most of the talking as he reminisced about his favorite Christmas memories. Lucas gave the large man the second half of his game hen before he starting in on his peach pie. Lucas took in small, slow forkfuls of the pie as he savored each bite.

After lunch, Lucas returned to his cell and laid down in his bunk. Steve's stories had gotten him thinking about his own holiday seasons over the years and he let his mind wonder down memory lane.

He remembered the first Christmas he and Sarah spent in their new house. They had chopped down and decorated a nice cedar tree a month before the big day. By the time Christmas rolled around, the neglected tree had completely shriveled up and had lost most of its needles. The brittle limbs could barely hold up any ornaments, but it still made them happy.

He recalled their first Christmas with new baby Mark. He was less than four months old, and they were still terrified and very sleep deprived. Thankfully, Lucas' sister spent the holidays with them that year, and she helped to take care of Mark while they rested.

He remembered the Christmas mornings he had spent with his grandchildren; his precious little Katie and Tyler. They were always so excited to open presents and run around the neighborhood showing off their new toys.

He played out every Christmas and New Year in his mind, going through each one year-by-year. There were so many wonderful memories that he couldn't allow himself to be sad. He had lived a blessed life, even given his current situation.

Lucas was about to move on and start reading a book when he realized he had missed one holiday memory. It was the memory of both his worst Christmas and best holiday season. How could he forget the first holiday he ever spent with Sarah?

Christmas in Japan

"Every man has his secret sorrows which the world knows not; and oftentimes we call a man cold when he is only sad."
— Henry Wadsworth Longfellow

Winter 1962

***

The area that is now Marine Corps Air Station Iwakuni, Japan has changed hands several times over the decades. It started as a Japanese naval air station in 1938 and served as the main base of operations for the planning of Japan's attack on Pearl Harbor. At the end of World War II, the base at Iwakuni was taken over by forces from the United States, Great Britain, Australia, and New Zealand. Soon after, the Royal Australian Air Force was given sole command of the base in 1948. The United States was invited to again establish a joint command on the base in 1950 during the Korean Conflict, and the United States eventually took over sole command in 1952. The base switched hands from the U.S. Air Force to the U.S Navy and eventually to the U.S. Marine Corps throughout the next decade, each time gaining more buildings, upgrades, and personnel. The installation officially became a Marine Corps Air Station in 1962, just seventeen years after the end of WWII, and it has remained under the command of the Marine Corps since that time.

***

Mail Call

Lucas lowered his head as he walked up the stairs leading into the main headquarters building. He hated going to HQ. The large old white building was filled with an assortment of officers that he had to greet at every turn. Plus, the building's sordid history gave him the creeps.

As Lucas walked the halls, he could still envision Admiral Yamamoto and his staff scurrying around the building planning the attack on Pearl Harbor. He had taken pride in being part of the dedication service earlier that year when the installation had become an official Marine Corps air station. That was one of the only positive things he could point to after spending just over a year at the secluded location.

Hostilities still ran deep with the locals in the town of Iwakuni, which was less than an hour's train ride away from Hiroshima. Service members at the air station were rarely allowed outside the gates, and on the rare occasions they were allowed off base, it was only for official functions and never for fun or sightseeing.

Lucas passed the admin office and finance center before entering the small post office at the end of the hall. He was pleased to see the familiar face of Lance Corporal Taddy Johnson, or Tadpole as everyone called him. Tadpole had arrived on the island about three months ago, and he was the newest edition to the small barracks crew that Lucas called friends.

Tadpole was a skinny young man just barely in his twenties. His hair was cut beyond regulation short making it look like he had a fuzzy horse shoe sitting on the crown of his head. He hailed from Boston, Massachusetts, a fact that he made sure to announce repeatedly every time he had a few drinks.

"Hey Tadpole. I hear you have a package for me."

"Hi Fosty… Er, I mean Corporal Fosterman," Tadpole stammered as he noticed his captain eying him from his corner office. "You got a big box here. And it's heavy too."

Tadpole stepped into the storage room and pulled out a large square cardboard box that must have been two feet in all directions. Lucas was surprised by the weight as he took it from Tadpole and sat it down on the counter. He smiled a bit when he noticed the name on the address label… Mister Glenn Fosterman, his father.

"What the heck is it," Tadpole asked.

"Oh just some junk I asked my dad to send me from home," replied Lucas, giving Tadpole a wink. "You'll have to stop by my room after work. We're planning on cooking up some steaks for Christmas Eve."

"Wouldn't miss it, Corporal," said Tadpole in a loud official sounding voice, causing his captain to smirk and roll his eyes.

The Package

"Guinness, man. Guinness. And Harps. And cigars. And they aren't the cheap ones either. And deer sausage. I can't believe my luck and the unbelievable generosity of my dear old dad," yelled Lucas to a young corporal who was looking in the barracks room window. He took off running for the building's main door.

Kelvin Goreman, or Kilgore as everyone called him, was a gangly young man, with red hair, a long face and curious eyes. He was a bit hyper active, but not in a completely annoying kind of way. Best of all he was the generous type and always willing to go the extra mile for the good of his fellow man.

A few seconds later Kilgore came bursting through the barracks room door, frantic and gleeful. He stopped short and stared in amazement at the bounty laid out neatly on the coffee table. A case of Guinness. A case of Harps. A sack of assorted cigars. Four sticks of deer sausage. A calendar filled with lively pin up gals. A Santa hat. Two cookie tins. A fancy gold cigar lighter with the words "Semper Fi Son" written on the side. And a copy of J.P Donleavy's *The Ginger Man*.

Lucas had been stuck on this God-forsaken island for too long, and it was about damn time things started going his way.

"My hell, how did your dad get all this through customs? It must have cost him a fortune to ship!" Kilgore was mystified.

"Hell if I know, but it's here now."

Both men stood in awe, blinking quietly at the pile of contraband. In the states, these items would have made superb Christmas presents for any single man, but here in mainland Japan, at a tiny air station clear across the Pacific Ocean, it was a damn miracle. Words couldn't describe the emotions they were feeling.

Sure, beer was plentiful in Japan, but it was mostly Sapporo and Kirin and other slop that resembled formaldehyde. Those beers were okay with sushi and for a quick fix, but not for real drinking. American standards like Bud, Miller, and such were sometimes available at the Package Store, but real Irish and English brews were nowhere to be found. Lucas had written home begging for a bottle or two of "good" beer and possibly a couple cigars to share, but this was a dream come true.

They stood in wonder a bit longer before processing the treasure. Lucas unwrapped the beer and placed it gingerly into a cooler, adjusting the ice at the bottom. Not too cold now.

Kilgore began inspecting the cigars one at a time. He smoothed down the loose edges and dusted off a few particles from one before placing it like a wounded bird into a small box.

Lucas grabbed the sausage links and placed them in the cooler. The cookies went into a lock box at the bottom of his wall locker, padlocked for security. He threw the lighter in his pocket, Santa hat on his head, and sat down and started thumbing through *The Ginger Man*.

"All right, I'm off to the store," said Kilgore clapping his hands together. "Let's see. We need some meat, a bag of potatoes, a proper ash tray, crackers, and five glasses. Anything else?"

"A Christmas tree if you can find one. It is Christmas Eve for Pete's sake."

"Right then. God bless." He said as he shot out the door.

He returned seconds later, already winded. "Crap man, does Bruno know?"

"Not yet. He is still at the gym killing the heavy bag. I'll catch him on his way in."

"Right, God bless."

Enter the Grump

Lucas passed the time by reading some passages from *The Ginger Man*. He was engrossed in a story about a wonderful sounding woman named Ginny Cupper.

"Hey slob, I missed ya' on da' playground." Bruno stood like an ox in the doorway.

Bruno was the resident thug. His real name was Roger Bruner, but everyone called him Bruno, mainly because he looked like a classic Bronx bruiser, complete with worn brown leather jacket and black watch cap. He spent two hours a day at the gym training to be the next heavyweight champion, even though he was only five-feet eight-inches tall and weighed 160 pounds. He wouldn't look a bit out of place playing a mob enforcer in a gangster movie. To complicate things, Bruno spoke with a thick southern accent, which didn't match his name, attitude, or look. At first glance everyone assumed he was from NY, but in reality, he was from Nashville, Tennessee.

"Who the hell wears a leather jacket to the gym?" Lucas retorted.

"It's cold out, damn it," he said with a scowl.

"It's 60 degrees out, and it makes you look like a pussy."

"Pussy my ass. Does this look like a pussy?" He said showing off one of his medium-size biceps.

"Screw that," Lucas changed the subject. "I've got something to show you. Take a look in the cooler."

Bruno gave him a wry look and haphazardly strolled over to the cooler. He opened it looking disinterested, but quickly realized what was inside.

"Holy Crap! 'Dat can't be real. Black Gold and Blondie. How on earth did ya' get 'dat?"

"From the Pops." Lucas smiled

"You, Fosty, are a legendary hero."

"A regular Achilles," Lucas offered.

Bruno's eyes widened, "If ya' got 'dat box, 'dat means the mail done got here."

Before Lucas could tell him that he had picked up the package at the post office, Bruno sprinted out of the room. He returned a few minutes later with a few letters in hand. He pulled off his watch cap and slumped down in a chair, dejected.

He tossed two letters at Lucas and slapped another letter on top of the cooler. Lucas looked over and saw that the other letter was addressed to Kilgore.

"Don't worry about it Bruno… I'm sure you'll get something soon. You know how crappy the mail delivery is in this place," Lucas said trying to make him feel better. "Look here, both of these letters are postmarked December fourteenth."

Bruno wasn't listening anymore, and Lucas knew it. The poor sap hadn't received any mail from home in almost a month, and it was driving the man crazy. Bruno had a hard shell, but life at this solitary duty station left everyone a bit lonelier inside than they cared to admit.

"Ah'right. I'm goin' to hit da' shower," Bruno declared. "Don't let Kilgore drink all da' damn booze before da' party."

Lucas waited for Bruno to leave before sorting through his two envelopes. The first one was from his brother. It would have to wait. The second letter was from Kentucky. He smiled knowing it was from Sarah Blackstone.

He had corresponded with Sarah several times over the past year, and his heart still leapt every time he received a letter from her. His head told him that she was little more than a very pretty pen pal at this point, but his heart (or more likely his imagination) told him that she might be his soul mate.

He opened the envelope and pulled out a photo. The picture showed a group of people standing under a large banner that read Merry Christmas from the Blackstone Oak Barrel Company. Sarah was standing in the middle of the picture, surrounded by her two younger brothers, three other young men, and two young women. One of the women Lucas recognized as a lady named Barbara. Sarah's mom was also pictured sitting in a rocking chair. The whole crew was wearing Christmas hats and decked out in holiday garb.

Seeing that everyone in the photo looked happy brought a smile to Lucas' face. The Blackstone family had gone through a lot the past year. Sarah's father, and the originator of the business, had died last October due to a heart attack. It took the family several months to recover from his death, and even longer to get things back up and running with the company. Sarah had sent Lucas regular letters detailing how things were progressing, and he was heartened after each letter to see how great she was doing as the new leader of the small business.

He studied the picture for a while imagining what it must be like to spend Christmas in Kentucky. He spent even more time looking at Sarah. Even though it had been over a year since he saw her last, she still looked as beautiful as he remembered.

He turned over the photo and read the message.

Sorry for the generic Christmas photo, but I thought you might like to see what us Southern Folk look like in our natural habitat. I hope you are finding some ways to have fun this Christmas in Japan. Stay safe and write me when you have some spare time.

Merry Christmas,
Sarah

Lucas turned the photo back over so he could look back at the image. Out of all the gifts he had received today, nothing could beat having a picture of Sarah to look at throughout the lonely Holidays.

A Fine Feast

Lucas, Kilgore, and Bruno stood around a small iron grill watching impatiently as their small strip steaks cooked over a tiny bed of coals. The deer sausage and crackers helped to keep everyone sustained while they waited.

They had decided to hold the Christmas Eve festivities outside in the barracks courtyard. The weather had been unseasonably warm and dry that week. It was almost 6 pm and the temperature was still nearly forty-five degrees.

The decorations had gone up in a flash. A two-foot tall Bonsai tree decorated with silver streamers and small gold balls served as a makeshift Christmas tree. A couple strings of red garland were tacked to the wall along with more silver streamers for effect. Even a few poorly wrapped presents sat beside the small tree.

A coffee table had been brought out and covered with a white sheet. A red candle served as the center piece. Kilgore set the table with a pack of holiday service ware he had found somewhere. Holly-covered plates, red forks, green knives, and fancy napkins. The dining room was ready.

Lucas pulled the meat off the grill, placing a small steak on each plate before reloading the grill for round two. Tadpole ran into the courtyard holding a plate of piping hot baked potatoes that had been roasting on a rack in the boiler room.

Finally, they were joined by an old timer they called Archie. Archibald Bowman joined the Marine Corps late in life, and at twenty-seven he was one old private. Lucas, Kilgore, and Bruno were seasoned corporals each with around three years under their belts and Tadpole had spent a year on a boat before ending up in Japan. Even still, Lucas was the oldest at twenty-two. Archie's age was exacerbated by the fact that he was already balding and had a few too many grey streaks for a man under thirty. It was amazing how rank made a person feel older, and everyone treated Archie like a younger brother.

"Say grace, Archie," said Bruno, slapping him upside the head.

They all bowed their heads as Archie started in on a long-winded prayer thanking God for everything that was good and right in the world. Even the usually impatient Bruno stayed quiet throughout the dissertation, in honor of Christmas and all. "Amen."

Before sitting down at the coffee table, Lucas turned to the cooler. The time had come.

He pulled out two bottles of Guinness and two bottles of Harps. Next, he grabbed five Mason jars that Kilgore had managed to procure to serve as mugs. First went the Harps; then the Guinness. He took his time during the process, while Bruno critiqued his every move.

"Ya' pourin' too fast. Don't let 'em mix. Too much head. Slow down, damn it!"

"Back off cocksucker or you'll be drinking Oriental pisswater!" Lucas growled at him, nudging him back with his elbow.

That shut him up for a minute, giving Lucas time to concentrate on finishing his task.

The deed was done.

They all stood back and admired the frosty "mugs" filled with the most beautiful black and tans ever poured… at least by an American, in Japan, on Christmas Eve, into quart jars.

"I think I'm going to cry." Archie sniffled.

"Shut up pussy. Who's goin' to make the toast?" grumbled Bruno.

"To our swift return to the Brave New World. May this island release us to the waiting arms of beautiful blondes with hefty bosoms and wealthy ex-husbands!" Kilgore lifted his mug.

"Here. Here."

They all sat around the table and began the holiday feast, feeling like Kings of old. God bless all the little people.

Still giddy from their recent meal the five men sat back, letting their food digest and enjoyed a second round of black and tans. Time for presents.

Lucas gave each of the guys their choice of cigar along with engraved metal flasks that read, "Long Live the Oriental Chain Gang."

They all lit up their cigars as Kilgore handed out small

packages. Archie and Tadpole received engraved Zippo lighters, while Lucas and Archie received fancy journals. The covers of the journals had been decorated by Kilgore, who was quite the artists, and featured cartoon images from some of their times together over the past year.

Bruno pulled out two bottles of Jack Daniels, slapped a bow on each and handed one to Archie and the other to Tadpole. "Here ya' go boys. The finest skunk water the great state of Tennessee has to offer. Now you gunna' have ta' share, but at least ya' can't say I ain't ever givin' ya' nothin'."

Bruno then got up and grabbed his leather jacket. He reached into one of the pockets and pulled out two brown paper bags. He handed a small one to Kilgore and a longer skinny one to Lucas.

Lucas was a bit surprised that Bruno had gotten them anything, and he was even more shocked when saw Kilgore unwrap his paper bag to find a gold pocket watch.

"Damn Bruno, this was your grandpa's pocket watch," said Kilgore. "I can't take this."

"Oh hog wash. It's nothin' but an old pocket watch. I never wear it, bein' that it's so fancy and all. Besides, you're the pretty one out 'ah all us."

For some unknown reason a chill ran down Lucas' spine as he looked down at the narrow package in his hands. He slowly unwrapped the bag revealing a large fixed bladed knife.

He recognized it immediately. It was a Randal Made Model 2 Fighting Stiletto. Probably the finest knife known to man. It had an eight inch blade that had been sharpened on both sides and a leather wrapped grip that had been lovingly polished and cared for over the years. Lucas knew that the knife had belonged to Bruno's father who had died during World War II. Lucas sat in stunned silence for over a minute before looking up at Bruno and shaking his head.

"Come on, damn it. Can't a man give another man a gift without all dis' fuss. Ya' been admirin' that pig sticker all year. The damn thing just depresses me. At least ya' might be gettin' some joy out of it."

"But this was your dad's prized possession," protested Lucas.

"I still got his dog tags. That's all I need. I'm tired of lugging all dis' junk around like portable tombstones."

"Well, crap," Tadpole exclaimed, breaking the tension. "I didn't get anybody anything."

"Figures, ya' cheap bastard," replied Bruno slapping him in the back. "I bet Archie didn't get us nothin' neither."

"I'll have you know I got you old men one of the finest gifts known to man!" Archie smiled as he produced a small black box. He opened it up and pulled out four ink pens. He studied each one intently before handing them to their new owners.

They each took their pen and studied the busty vixens pictured on the barrel. For Kilgore it was a dark-haired Asian in a blue one-piece bathing suit, for Bruno a red-headed Irishwoman in a pretty green dress, for Lucas a blonde Midwestern gal in cutoff shorts and white t-shirt, for Tadpole a shirtless surfer dude in swimming trunks.

The four men looked at each other knowingly and turned their pens upside down watching as the clothes magically melted away. They all had a good laugh.

"Well Tadpole, since you are the cheap one you get to share your present first. Go grab some coffee cups from the break room." Kilgore commanded.

As Tadpole ran off, Lucas poured another round of black and tans. He handed the first one to Bruno declaring him the man of the hour and the best damn gift giver in the land.

Bruno just grumbled and took a long pull from his Mason jar.

Tadpole came back with a collection of coffee cups to pass around and started pouring generous shots of whiskey.

The men spent the rest of the evening telling stories from their best Christmas times at home. They polished off all but two of the Guinness, two of the Harps and half the second bottle of Jack.

At midnight, the sergeant on duty came by to announce lights out. "Come on guys, it's time for lights out. You don't want Santa to pass you by now do you?"

Without protest, the partygoers agreed that it was time to close down for the night. They took one last shot together, wished each other a Merry Christmas and headed off to bed.

An Un-Merry Christmas

Lucas knew all too well that the holidays were never the same away from home, and being in Japan with a group of other lonely souls made it all the more unbearable.

To fight off the impending gloom, he had convinced his small group of friends to go to the Christmas Day chapel service at noon. He met Kilgore in the hallway at 10 am to head to the mess hall for a late breakfast. They met Tadpole on the way out and knocked on Bruno and Archie's doors, but no one answered. The gym rats were probably already working out.

Lucas started the morning with a pounding headache, but two glasses of water and a heavy dose of shit-on-a-shingle made him feel like a new man. Kilgore was still looking a bit green as he picked at his food. Tadpole was barely twenty and had the constitution of a rhino. He was just plain giddy as he shoveled down his plate of SOS and convinced Kilgore to give him the rest of his.

The three men made their way back to the barracks to clean up. Lucas had just finished showering and was putting on his slacks and dress shirt when he got a knock at the door. He threw open the door and saw that it was Archie, already dressed in his Sunday finest.

Lucas grabbed his tie, slipped it around his neck, and started tightening the knot. "I'm glad to see that someone is ready to go on time. Where's Bruno?"

Not getting an answer, Lucas looked back at Archie and noticed that he was as pale as ghost. "What the hell, Archie? What's wrong?"

Archie didn't say a word. He just motioned for Lucas to follow him. They walked across the hallway and into Archie's room. Lucas turned and walked into the bathroom that Archie shared with Bruno. As soon as Lucas entered the bathroom he could see that the door leading into Bruno's room was open. For the second day in a row, a chill ran down his spine.

Lucas slowly walked across the bathroom and braced himself against the door frame before turning to look into the room.

Bruno was hanging from a rope in the center of the room. His face and neck were swollen and purple, and it was obvious that he had been hanging there for several hours. Dangling from his neck were two sets of dog tags. One were Bruno's, and Lucas knew the other pair belonged to Bruno's father. On the bed lay one open letter and one sealed letter with the name Tonya written on the back. Tonya was Bruno's wife.

"Damn it, Bruno," whispered Kilgore.

Lucas turned to see that Kilgore had entered the room and was standing next to him. They stood together in silence for a few seconds before Lucas choked back a few tears and turned to Archie.

"Go get the Duty. Kilgore, let's get him down from there."

It took everything Lucas had to lift Bruno's limp body high enough for Kilgore to remove the noose from around his neck. They had just lowered Bruno to the ground when Sergeant Landis walked in. "Son of a biscuit!"

A Lousy Service

Lucas stared at himself in the mirror. He had been standing there for five minutes trying to get his tie right. Finally happy with the knot he decided to give himself a thorough inspection. He was wearing his Class A service uniform. Green trousers, khaki long-sleeve button-up shirt, khaki tie, black shoes, green coat, and khaki web belt. The coat was form fitting and adorned with the few ribbons and marksmanship badges he had earned over the past three years.

He was surprised at how old he looked. He was only twenty-two, but he seemed to have developed several new lines around his eyes over the past several months. His brown hair had somehow darkened. His mother would tell him that he was still too thin and much too serious. He was convinced that the island somehow sucked the life out people, and it had certainly sunk its teeth into poor Bruno.

He straightened his web belt and grabbed his cover before heading out. As he walked out the barracks door, he saw Kilgore standing under the awning fixing Tadpole's tie. Archie came driving up in a jeep and offered everyone a lift. The four men climbed in and headed out to the chapel.

The service was short and sterile. The chaplain read a few familiar passages and said the typical prayers. There was no personality to it, nothing that Bruno would have approved of. Of course, Bruno would not have approved of any service at all. He hated any kind of attention. But the command had decided that they needed to do something in response, more as a preventative measure to ensure others didn't follow Bruno's lead.

After the service, the four men gathered in Lucas' room sitting quietly for a long while.

"Why did I have to give him that damn letter," said Tadpole breaking the silence. It turned out that Tadpole had hand delivered a letter that Bruno had received on Christmas Eve. He knew Bruno had been desperately waiting for a letter from home, and he wanted to surprise him with it when he got off work.

"How were you supposed to know it was a 'Dear John' letter?" Lucas shook his head. "I just can't believe we couldn't read the signs. Those damn gifts he gave us were just plain obvious."

"Screw that... I'm not going to blame myself or any of you," said Kilgore showing a flash of anger. "Bruno took the coward's way out. The selfish bastard."

"Man, that's harsh." Archie stared wide-eyed at Kilgore.

"No, he's right," said Lucas. "Bruno just kept it all inside and let the loneliness get to him. We all did the best we could to be his friends, but he wouldn't let us in most of the time. Hell, I didn't even know he was married until a few weeks ago."

"I can't wait to get off this damn island." Kilgore wiped away a tear.

"I'll drink to that." Lucas stood up to open the cooler. He poured five jars of black and tans, and the four men drank in silence watching the bubbles cascade in Bruno's glass.

A Strange Morning

The next morning Lucas was woken up early by the corporal on duty. "Hey Fosty, sorry to bug you, but the colonel wants to see you. His driver will be here in half an hour to pick you up."

"What the hell for?"

"Beats me. I'm just the messenger."

Lucas scrambled to his feet and jumped in the shower. He threw on his long-sleeve khaki shirt, green slacks, and tie before heading down to the break room to grab some coffee. He quickly downed a cup trying to wash away the cobwebs in his head.

He stood impatiently outside the front of the barracks waiting for the driver. He considered walking the half mile to the headquarters building, but decided that he should probably just let things play out. A few minutes later, the driver pulled up in front of the barracks.

"Hey Joe, how's it going." Lucas nodded to the driver as he climbed into the passenger seat.

"It's been a busy night. And before you ask, I don't know what the heck is going on or what the heck the CO wants with you. I was just told to come and get you. He's had the sergeant major in his office all night, along with guys from flight ops, admin folks, finance guys, and a bunch of other people."

Joe pulled up in front of the headquarters building and barely let Lucas out before hitting the gas. "Sorry to run, but I've got to get to the chapel to pick up Bruno's casket. I'll be back to get you in a few minutes."

Lucas was stunned as he looked up the stairs at the large old white headquarters building. There was only one way he was going to find out what the hell was going on.

Reporting as Ordered

Lucas entered Colonel Rider's office, stood at attention and announced, "Corporal Fosterman reporting as ordered."

"At ease Corporal," said the colonel not looking up from the letter he was writing. The colonel was a tall man with perfectly combed black hair and an overall polished look. Lucas always thought he looked like more of a friendly movie star version of an officer than the real thing, but he preferred that to the some of the grumps he had served under in the past.

Lucas looked over and saw Sergeant Major Jackson talking on the phone. The bulky man looked serious, like always, but he gave Lucas a quick nod. That set Lucas at ease a bit. The sergeant major was not a man that normally made friendly gestures.

"Sit down son," said Colonel Rider which grabbed Lucas' attention. Lucas sat down and placed his cover on his lap.

"I understand you were friends with Corporal Bruner. I'm sorry about his loss. We all are."

"Yes, sir." Lucas was suddenly feeling a bit out of place.

"I'm sure your wondering what you're doing here. Well, it turns out that Corporal Bruner's mother is a politician of some prominence in Nashville, and she is understandably upset about her son's passing. She has demanded that we get her son home rather quickly, and the higher ups have made it clear that we are to comply with her request ASAP."

The colonel finished the letter he was writing and stuffed it in an envelope before sealing it. He wrote "Mrs. Bruner" on the top and stuffed it in a folder on his desk.

"So that's where you come in. You have been at this station the longest out of all the enlisted men and are due for a change in assignment. I need someone to escort Corporal Bruner's body back home, and it looks like you are the man for the job."

The colonel stood up and handed Lucas the folder. "We've been up all night making the arrangements. Admin has put together your new orders. You are to report to Alameda California to join the crew of the USS Midway by March first. You have over sixty days of leave on the books, so you might as well use it up. You probably won't get much of a chance to take leave once you get on the boat, especially with things heating up in Vietnam like they are."

"Finance has cut you an advance on your pay, and I'm sure you have plenty of cash squirreled away after living on this rock for the past year. God knows there isn't anywhere to spend it in this place."

Colonel Rider stood up and waved the sergeant major over to join them. Lucas instinctively stood up and looked around confused.

"I wish we had more time to do this formally, but we are running out of time. You have to catch a plane in about three hours, and you still have to get your uniforms in order, pack up, and get some paperwork done." The colonel nodded to the sergeant major.

The sergeant major walked up to Lucas and handed him a few packages of chevrons and a certificate announcing that he had been promoted to the rank of sergeant. He also gave him a couple of assorted medals and ribbons before shaking his hand and grumbling, "Congratulations, son."

Lucas was surprised by the sudden promotion. He knew he was due for an increase in rank sooner than later, but the makeshift ceremony came as a bit of a shock. He looked down at the ribbons in his hand. He recognized an overseas service ribbon and meritorious unit commendation. These were routinely given to Marines leaving the island. He also saw a Navy Commendation Medal, which was a surprise. His time in Japan had gone well, but he was not expecting to receive any type of medal. He started to ask about it, but the sergeant major was already shoving more paperwork into his hands.

"Now the driver will meet you outside to take you over to your room. Mama San Ogana will meet you at the barracks to get your uniforms fixed up while you pack. You'll need to turn in your pistol and badge at the armory before heading over to the airfield. Flight ops has set up a flight for you to Okinawa where you will jump on a C-130 headed directly to Nashville," said the colonel, again nodding at the sergeant major.

"Look son, I need to you understand this," started the sergeant major looking very stern. "Once you get on that plane, you are one-hundred percent responsible for getting Corporal Bruner's body back to Nashville. You are never to leave that casket. You will eat, sleep, and piss within eyesight of that casket. If the plane breaks down or even gets shot down, you will not leave that casket. Do you understand?"

Lucas nodded.

The sergeant major handed Lucas a folded up American flag wrapped in plastic. "Once you arrive in Nashville, you will drape this flag over the casket. An Honor Guard will meet you at the airport in Nashville and serve as pallbearers. You will make sure that the flag is folded properly and hand it over to Missus Bruner along with that letter from the colonel. You will salute her and tell her that you are sorry for her loss. Do you understand?"

"I understand," lied Lucas. He did not understand any of it. His head was still spinning.

"All right then, get your skinny butt out of here," said the sergeant major. "I will meet you on the flight line in three hours. Make sure you get something to eat. It's going to be a long flight."

The colonel walked around the desk and shook Lucas' hand. "It's been a pleasure serving with you sergeant. I wish your duty here could have ended on a happier note. Best of luck on the high seas."

Lucas snapped a quick salute, executed an about face, and retreated out of the office. As he walked down the hall he saw Tadpole standing in the doorway of the post office looking anxious. "What the hell is going on?"

"I've been given orders to take Bruno home. Then I'm going to California to catch a boat."

"Holy crap. When do you leave?"

"In three hours. I'm going back to pack up now."

"Damn Fosty, I'm sorry we didn't get to send you off properly. Best of luck."

"You take care of Archie and Kilgore, and don't let this rock take you down." Lucas waved a final goodbye.

Farewell and Goodbye

Lucas was almost done packing his sea bag when Kilgore showed up at his door. "Tadpole said you got orders."

"I've been ordered to take Bruno home to Nashville, then I get sixty days leave before checking into the *USS Midway* out of Cali."

"That is crazy man. And you're leaving today?"

"Joe here is driving me around to finish my checkout. I have to be on the plane in less than two hours." Lucas nodded at Joe who had just walked up behind Kilgore holding an assortment of uniforms.

"Here you go Sarge. Mama San sewed everything on, pressed them out, and even put on your new medals."

"Thanks Joe." Lucas slipped on one of the khaki long-sleeve shirts and placed the other uniform pieces in a garment bag.

Kilgore grabbed Lucas' sleeve. "Sergeant? Damn man, you have had a busy morning. Promotion, orders, new medals, sixty days of leave, and a flight off the rock."

"Tell me about it. I guess Bruno's mom is some bigwig in Nashville and the top brass want him brought home in a hurry."

"Well man I hate to see you go, but I'll be right on your heels. I've been here almost as long as you have, so my time is coming."

"Tell Archie I said goodbye," Lucas slipped on his tie and straitened it in the mirror. He threw his sea bag over to Joe and zipped up his garment bag. He gave his room one last look and headed to the door. He stopped in front of Kilgore and gave him a quick hug. "I couldn't have made it through the past year without you Kilgore. You have been a great drinking buddy and even better friend."

With that, Lucas headed out of the barracks and jumped into the jeep.

One Long Flight

Lucas sat in the webbed basket seat of a C-130 looking over at Bruno's large black casket. It was a fancy box that had a glossy lacquered finish and brass hardware. He was glad to finally be in the air again after dealing with the transfer in Okinawa. The final leg of his journey would take him nearly fifteen hours with one stopover for fuel in Hawaii along the way.

He was alone in the cargo bay of the plane. The aircraft's small crew consisted of only two pilots up front and one crew chief, who also stayed in front out of respect for the dead. A heavy black curtain divided the cargo bay from the rest of the plane.

Lucas was relieved to be by himself. He needed time to process everything and decide what to do next. He hadn't even read over his new orders yet or decided what to do with his time off. He knew he needed to go home and see his family, but there was no way he was going to spend sixty days at home.

Reading over his orders, he found out that he was going to be the senior enlisted man for the Marine Security Guard Attachment aboard the *USS Midway*. That explained the quick promotion.

Apparently, the boat had just gotten back from a tour and wasn't due to leave for another deployment unit later next year. Lucas wondered what security duty would be like aboard a docked aircraft carrier.

He pulled out the envelope he had received from finance and looked over the check. He was surprised by the number. They had paid him at his new rank, which was nice. The check covered ten weeks of pay plus travel expenses and per diem for his trip from Nashville to Alameda. Plus, he already had a decent nest egg saved up from spending the last year on the island.

His options for leave had just increased a bit, now that he had some real spending cash. He chuckled to himself as he realized he knew exactly where his first stop would take him… Louisville, Kentucky.

Lucas slept for most of the first leg of the flight, enjoying the peace and quiet. He never had reason to leave the cargo bay since he had been given a sack full of boxed lunches. A honey pot sat in the corner for bathroom breaks. From time to time he would read a little from his copy of *The Ginger Man*, but mostly he just slept and thought about the future and about seeing Sarah again.

The stopover in Hawaii was uneventful, with the whole evolution taking less than an hour. The crew chief had only briefly made an appearance at the curtain to deliver a hot meal of fried chicken and corn on the cob from the Air Ops cafeteria.

He also handed Lucas two Cokes. "Everything okay back here Sergeant Fosterman?" He was obviously not comfortable being so close to a casket.

"Everything is fine." Lucas handed the crew chief a bag of trash.

"Well if you need anything just yell up front."

"Thank you, but I'll be fine."

Lucas waited for the aircraft to takeoff and reach altitude before digging into his lunch. He suddenly felt guilty for enjoying a plate full of fried chicken next to the casket. Bruno absolutely loved fried chicken and never missed an opportunity to eat multiple plates whenever it was served at the chow hall.

He finished his lunch and settled back in for another nap. After a few hours he took out the Christmas photo Sarah had sent him. He let his mind wonder back to the first time he had ever seen her in that high-rise hotel bar in Tacoma just over a year ago.

He could still picture her wearing that simple black dress with her jet black hair and bright hazel eyes. He had spent a magical day with her, but their time together was cut short when she had to catch a flight home to see her father who had suffered a heart attack. Her dad managed to hang on until she got home, but died a few days later leaving Sarah as the new head of the household and business.

He stuffed the photo back into his pocket and laid back again to close his eyes. Throughout the rest of the trip he alternated between day dreams and napping as he tried to calm his nerves.

His stomach churned a bit when he heard the engines change speed and felt the plane begin to descend. He was dreading the next part of his mission. He started fidgeting with his uniform, fixed his hair, and even buffed out his shoes for the third time. He grabbed the folded flag and unwrapped the plastic cover. He didn't know how long he had to prepare the casket and he wanted to be ready.

The plane landed a few minutes later, and the crew chief stuck his head through the curtain. "Hey, Sarge. The pilot is going to keep the cargo bay closed until you give the word. I am going to run out and make sure the Honor Guard is ready to go."

Lucas looked out the window and saw five cars parked beside an open hanger. He was relieved to see that the weather was cooperating. There wasn't any rain and there was still at least an hour of daylight left.

He quickly unfolded the flag and draped it over the casket. He wasn't happy to see that there were so many creases and wrinkles showing. He worked feverishly to smooth it out as best he could. After a couple of minutes, he was glad to see that the flag started to lay flat.

The crew chief popped his head back in and said that the Honor Guard was ready. Lucas stood up and straightened his uniform. He placed his cover on his head and gave the crew chief a nod.

Lucas stood behind the casket as the cargo bay door opened, creating a ramp. He could see the Honor Guard standing in front of him. As soon as the door settled open, Lucas gave the men a nod, and they started marching up the ramp. The men lifted the heavy casket and silently started their march toward the open hangar. Lucas followed close behind trying to match his steps with the steps of the Honor Guard.

They entered the hangar and Lucas could see about a dozen people watching as the casket was placed in the back of an open hearse. The Honor Guard silently removed and folded the flag, while Lucas used his peripheral vision to scan the crowd. He saw Missus Bruner standing in a puffy fur coat wiping away tears with a handkerchief. She was standing in front of the group with other family members placing hands on her shoulders for support. Unfortunately, she had been through this drill before with Bruno's father, so she knew what was coming.

Lucas tried to look through the rest of the crowd to see if he could see Bruno's wife. He wondered if she was there. *What did she look like? Did she know how much pain she had caused him?*

Lucas was handed the flag, and he slowly walked over to Missus Bruner. He handed her the flag and spoke as clearly as he could muster, "On behalf of a grateful nation, we are sorry for your loss."

He also handed her the letter from Colonel Rider. She looked at Lucas for a few seconds before offering him a slight smile. "Thank you for bringing my son home."

With that the family walked away and got in their vehicles.

Lucas stood and watched them leave feeling a bit guilty. He felt like he should have said more. He wanted to let Missus Bruner know that her son was his friend and that he was sorry that he couldn't stop him from taking his own life. But he knew none of that mattered now. It was better this way.

"Okay Sergeant, I guess we are all done here," said the corporal in charge of the Honor Guard. "You need a ride somewhere?"

Lucas snapped out of his haze and looked back at the corporal. "Yeah, it would be great if you could give me a lift to the bus station. I need to catch a bus to Louisville."

"I can take you," said another corporal from the group. "I'm driving down to Lexington tonight if you want a lift."

"That would be swell!" Lucas smiled. "Just let me grab my stuff."

He ran to the C-130 and grabbed his sea bag and uniforms. He said a quick goodbye to the pilots and crew chief and headed back to the corporal who had opened the trunk of his 1955 Chevy Impala. Lucas threw in his luggage and climbed into the passenger seat.

"Thank you, Corporal," said the grateful sergeant. "I am ready to get as far away from this place as possible."

An Unexpected Visitor

Sarah Blackstone had her black hair pulled back in a ponytail, and she was wearing a full-length blacksmith apron. Her face, neck, and arms were coated in a thick mix of sweat and brown dirt.

She had been hammering thin strips of metal sheet into barrel hoops for almost three hours now. Even still, she was able to work at a swift and steady pace moving from one side of the anvil to the other pounding away with her cross-peen hammer.

Sarah normally worked in the main office handling sales and

making business decisions, but during this year's holiday season she had decided to give everyone the week off between Christmas and the New Year's Day. With everyone gone it gave her a chance to spend time out in the workshop getting reacquainted with her barrel making skills. It was now three days after Christmas and this was the first day that she had found a chance to visit the workshop.

She finished another hoop and tossed it into a bin holding more than thirty finished rings before grabbing another long piece of sheet metal.

She looked up as she started to move toward the anvil and saw a tall, thin man standing at the front of the workshop. He looked like a vision as the sun backlit him creating a silhouette. She could tell that he was wearing a military uniform. She let the hammer hang down to her side and smiled.

"You told me to stop by Kentucky if I ever had some spare time," said Lucas. "So this is what you look like in your natural habitat."

Prison Life – Year Nine

"At his best, man is the noblest of all animals; separated from law and justice he is the worst."

– Aristotle

***

Hector Morales had grown up in northern Colombia. His mother, father, two brothers, and Hector had all been forced to work for the Romero drug cartel.

His mother and father worked for years in the conversion house, which was responsible for converting coca leaves into cocaine paste. This was a nasty process that involved soaking coca leaves in a mixture of sodium carbonate and water before adding kerosene to the mix. His parents would then stomp on the leaves to separate the chemicals before draining off the horrible smelling liquid. The mixture was put through a few more steps and a lengthy drying process before becoming a cocaine paste. This paste served as the base for creating a variety of different highly profitable and highly sought after recreational drugs.

Hector and his older brother, Juan, had been forced to work in the harvest fields as soon as they were able to carry baskets of coca leaves. Their youngest brother, Miguel, was still a toddler when Hector turned eight and started working the fields.

He hated the cartel and everything it represented. He hated that his father and mother had to work in the conversion house. He hated the sickly smell of coca leaves and kerosene that permeated the small one-room hut they lived in. He hated the drunken thugs that policed their small work camp twenty-four hours a day. He hated everything about his life.

Hector's older brother, on the other hand, fully embraced life in the cartel. He had also started working in the harvest fields at age eight and was promoted to supervisor by age twelve. After a few years, he was put in charge of the packaging center, where he became known for his ruthless efficiency and harsh management style. From that position he had a direct line to Rudy Romero, the undisputed head of the Romero Cartel.

When Hector turned fourteen, Juan recommended him for a position at the Romero mansion. Hector was not excited to begin working more closely with the cartel thugs, but he was relieved to no longer be slaving away in the fields or working in any of the horrid processing houses.

After a long lecture from Juan about not causing trouble for the family, Hector reported to the Romero mansion, which was run by Rudy's wife, Mariana. She was a stern woman in her mid-fifties who had little tolerance for laziness and absolutely zero patience. She was a tall, slender lady with dark black hair, brown eyes and a rigid demeanor. She was pretty for her age, especially when compared to the few other women at the compound.

Hector was assigned to the car and boat garage where he cleaned and serviced a small fleet of cars, trucks, and boats. The front of the garage had twelve vehicle bays that held an assortment of high-end sedans, work trucks, and a couple American muscle cars. The back of the garage housed four indoor boat slips. Each slip housed a luxury speed boat; the smallest being around forty feet long and the largest sitting at just over sixty feet.

He liked spending time in the large garage because there usually wasn't anyone around to hassle him. He even slept in the garage in case his services were needed at night, and he enjoyed spending quiet evenings sitting on the boat dock looking out at the Gulf of Mexico.

After three years, Hector was promoted to driver. Mariana liked using him as her driver because he was always on time and hardly ever spoke. Plus, Hector was a sharp looking young man who looked professional in a suit.

Hector's younger brother, Miguel, took over his duties in the garage. Hector was happy that he got to spend his evenings with his brother. Since starting work in the garage he had only gotten to see his family on random Sundays, and even then it was only for a few hours. Once Miguel started working in the garage, they got to spend nearly every evening together.

Hector didn't mind driving for Mariana because it usually took him away from the ugliness of the drug world. He spent most of his days driving her and her friends around the city of Barranquilla to stores, restaurants, hair salons, spas, and other fancy places. Every few weeks he also got a chance to skipper the women to Aruba on a forty-two-foot speed boat.

While in Aruba, the woman usually spoke English, and Mariana made it clear that she wanted him to learn the language as well for some reason. Hector spent a large portion of his downtime going through the translation programs that Mariana had purchased for him to listen to on an MP3 player. Miguel would usually join Hector in his lessons at night and the two young men would speak to each other in English whenever they were alone together as practice.

During his daily runs Hector learned a lot about cartel business listening to Mariana. He overheard conversations about finances, upcoming shipments, rival drug lords, and a host of other issues. He also learned the private details of the Romero family. He knew about Rudy Romero's erectile issues, his love for military arms (especially sniper rifles), his disdain for American culture, even about the ugly birthmark on his chest that he hated so much.

Hector's cushy job came to an end when the cartel's main drug runner, Marco, was killed by a rival cartel while on his way to deliver a shipment somewhere near Texas. Rudy had heard good things from Mariana about Hector's ability to speak English and pilot a Regal 42 Sport Coupe speedboat, so he tapped him as the new delivery boy.

Rudy was especially on edge after losing such a large shipment of drugs. His operation was already hemorrhaging cash due to rival competitors and a horrible coca crop yield that year. This made the latest loss even more painful. For the next two weeks, the production house workers were pushed past the point of exhaustion. Juan's crews had to work day and night to package a new shipment. Everyone in the camp felt pressured to calm their irritable leader.

Hector was scared witless when the time came to leave. Rudy, along with Mariana and Juan, met him at the dock to go over everything one last time. The plan was simple. Hector was to sail the boat to Louisiana to a place called Bay Chaland near the town of Cocodrie. There he was to meet a man named Jean Paul who would be waiting with a minivan. The two men would load the vehicle and drive it to a little farm just outside Kansas City where they would make the final delivery. Jean Paul would then return Hector to the boat for the trip back to Colombia.

As Hector entered the coordinates into the GPS, Rudy met him on the boat. He went below deck and looked over the shipment one last time before coming back topside to review the GPS coordinates.

He turned to look directly into Hector's eyes and stared at him for a few silent, uncomfortable moments. It was clear he was sizing up Hector to be absolutely sure he was ready for the job. Hector was absolutely sure that he was not ready for the job, but it was too late for that now. Finally, Rudy broke eye contact and gave Hector a slight smile.

"You'll be fine boy," he said in perfect English, another test. "But I need for you to understand how important this shipment is to me and our little family here. How important it is to you and your family," he said putting his arm around Hector. "If my shipment does not make it to its destination, then I will be forced to kill your father and your mother. I don't mean this as a threat, it is simply business."

Hector knew this to be true because he had witnessed Rudy personally murder Marco's mother just two weeks ago after the loss of the last shipment.

"If my shipment does arrive, but you decide you want to stay in America… then I will only kill your mother." Rudy smiled again and slapped Hector on the back. "Good luck boy. See you in a couple of days."

The first leg of the journey went smoothly. He crossed the Gulf of Mexico without even seeing another ship. It wasn't until he was a few miles from Louisiana that he saw another boat, a heavily loaded shipping barge. He watched as it continued its eastward journey toward New Orleans.

Once he was sure he was alone again, he powered the boat to the mouth of Bay Chaland. It was almost 10 am when he pulled into the bay. He turned on the blue and green lights at the front of the boat, which was the signal for Jean Paul. A few minutes later he saw two quick white flashes coming from a dock on his left side. He steered the boat into the dock where a tall, lanky Frenchman was waiting for him.

The two men didn't say a word upon meeting each other. They just nodded their hellos and used hand signals when needed. It took them almost half an hour to move the heavy sacks of drugs from the lower deck to the silver minivan.

Hector secured the boat before jumping into the passenger side of the van. He was exhausted from the stressful trip. He laid back in the seat and closed his eyes for a bit.

He woke a while later when he felt the van slow down as it began to exit a freeway. He looked up to see that they were pulling into a truck stop in a town called Springfield, Missouri.

"Ya' wanna' pop boy?" Jean Paul broke the silence. These were the first words Hector heard from him, and he was taken back by his thick Cajun accent.

"What?" Replied Hector, not understanding him.

"Ya' wanna' pop or some water?"

"Water would be good." Hector sat up and stretched his stiff muscles.

Jean Paul started the gas pump and headed into the store. Hector was still a bit numb from the trip and the events leading up to it. His nerves were still on edge as he looked around at the other cars at the pumps and scanned the parking lot.

He noticed two black cars that looked odd to him for some reason. They were sitting away from the other vehicles in the lot. He could see from their exhaust that both were still running.

Jean Paul got back in the van and handed Hector a bottle of water. Hector nodded at the two black cars. "Yup, I saw them." Jean Paul sounded calm.

They pulled out of the parking lot and headed North on Highway 65. Jean Paul started at an even 60 miles an hour keeping a watchful eye on the rearview mirrors. Hector also looked closely at the mirrors and could see two sets of headlights following at a slight distance.

After about twenty miles, Jean Paul decided to push the speed a bit getting up to 85 in the straightaways. At this speed, he should have been pulling away from the two cars, but they were obviously not falling away. Hector could see beads of sweat pool on Jean Paul's forehead. Jean Paul reached into the center console and pulled out a black pistol.

"Sorry boy, I only got one." He shrugged, and pushed the speed up another notch. Hector's heart started racing, and he began craning his neck around looking for their obvious pursuers.

About three minutes later, they came upon a sharp curve. The van's tires squealed loudly as Jean Paul struggled to keep the vehicle on the road. After making it through the curve Jean Paul barely tapped the breaks before yanking the wheel hard to the right to make a sharp turn onto a county dirt road. The minivan went up on two wheels and nearly tipped over, but Jean Paul managed to get it under control. He drove about a quarter mile down the dusty road before it dead ended at a chained cattle gate.

Jean Paul threw the vehicle into park, shut off the headlights, and turned off the engine. Hector spun around in his seat to look back at the entrance to the dirt road. The two men waited in silence for what seemed like an eternity. Finally, they saw one set of headlights speed by. A few seconds later a second set of headlights flew by. Both men let out huge sighs and started to laugh.

Hector slumped back in his seat slapping his chest in an effort to slow his racing heart rate. Jean Paul crossed his arms over the steering wheel and put his head down. They sat there quietly for another ten minutes.

Finally, Jean Paul shifted back up in his seat and grabbed the keys. He was just about to start the ignition when the blinding glare of two headlights shined in the mirrors.

Jean Paul looked over at Hector and smirked. "Wait here, boy. I got this."

Hector watched as he jumped out of the minivan with pistol in hand. He turned and looked straight ahead at the shiny red gate. He could hear shouting from Jean Paul and at least two other men, then gun shots, then more shouting from the other men who were not Jean Paul.

Hector kept looking straight ahead at the shiny red gate. He started to cry, slowly at first, then harder as the men approached and the shouting got louder. He wasn't crying because he was going to prison. He had lived as a prisoner all his life. He was crying because he knew that he had failed. He knew that he had killed his mother and his father.

***

One Young Fish

Lucas and the rest of the prison crew that worked in the Graybar Penitentiary woodshop were just getting back from lunch. It was only Wednesday, but they were already behind on their quota for the week. The current order was for thirty footlockers and the crew was down from the normal thirteen men to just eleven.

Lucas' most reliable crewmember, James, was serving two weeks in the hole for fighting, and he had lost another decent craftsman to discharge on Monday.

Normally, he would just buckle down and personally knock out a few footlockers to get the order back on track. But he hadn't been feeling well the past few days, and his stomach constantly ached. He planned to visit the infirmary, but he wanted to wait until Friday after the shipment was picked up.

As soon as the men started back to work, lead guard Jerry walked into the workshop pushing a young Hispanic prisoner in front of him. "Hey Fosty, I got a fish for you. I don't know how much help he will be. He looks afraid of his own shadow, and I don't think he knows much English. But at least he's another body. Maybe you can use him as a lumper until he figures things out."

"Thanks boss." Lucas stood up to look over the young man. "I can use all the help I can get this week."

Lucas winced as he moved toward the young man, and he could see that Jerry had noticed the twinge of pain cross his face. "What is your name?" Lucas hurriedly asked, trying to avoid any questions from the guard.

"My nobre es Hector, Hector Morales." The man's voice was soft.

"Hello Hector. I am Lucas Fosterman, but everyone here calls me Fosty."

"That's 'Mister Fosty' to you," a gruff looking prisoner

behind Lucas named Frank growled. Frank was member of a biker gang on the outside, and he led a small gang of other bikers on the inside. He was a hulking man with large arms that barely fit into his gray t-shirt. He sported a goatee that extended down about eight inches.

"Si. Yes, sir. Mister Fosty."

"Well, I am sure you will fit in just fine. Go ahead and pull out some sand paper from the cabinet in the far corner, medium one-hundred grit, and we will get you started."

Lucas watched the tall, skinny young man cross the room. The newbie kept his head low, making sure not to make eye contact with the other inmates.

"He just got off the bus," said Jerry. "He's going to have a tough time if he doesn't start puffing out his chest. He's too young and pretty to be acting like a sissy in this place."

Lucas nodded his head in agreement and sat back down on his stool. He winced hard as he bent at the waste and let out a grunt.

"What's going on with you Fosty?" Jerry sounded worried. "Did you get in a scuffle or something? These guys better not be causing you any problems."

"No, nothing like that. Just a little stomach trouble. It should pass in a few days. If it is still giving me problems on Friday I will get it checked out."

"All right then. I'll let you get back to it."

Back to Work

Lucas decided it would be easiest to have Hector shadow him for the rest of the day as he ran from station to station inspecting footlockers and barking out orders. He was relieved to discover that the young man understood everything he said. His poor English appeared to be more a product of shyness than a lack of knowledge.

At around three o'clock the two men found themselves working together sanding on a footlocker.

"So where are you from son?"

"I am from Colombia, Mister Fosty."

"That's one place I have never been. I hear it is a beautiful country."

"Si, muy hermoso."

"Hector, I am not sure why you are hiding your English skills, but I suppose you have your reasons."

"I just do not want to be noticed. I prefer to keep to myself and be left alone."

"Son, that may work for an old man like me. No one cares about geriatrics and I am not a threat to anyone. But you are too young to try to go it alone in this place. You need to pick a family and stick with them for protection. Otherwise, you are going to become a victim."

"Thank you Mister Fosty," Hector looked away. "I have already lost my family, and I am not ready to join another one."

Lucas didn't know how to respond to the curious statement. He could tell the man was hurting, so he decided to let it go. He figured the young fish would just have to learn the hard way how life works Graybar.

A Long Night

Lucas had been given permission from the lead evening guard to skip dinner and head to his cell. He was exhausted. His stomach was really hurting now, and he felt a constant stabbing sensation on the lower right side of his abdomen.

He was relieved that they had finished half the footlockers by the end of the day. Plus, the crew was in mid-construction on the rest of the order. He knew Thursday would be a hard day of work, but the goal was back within reach.

Hector had proven to be a quick learner with a good eye for

detail. Lucas just hoped he would prove as resourceful at fitting in with the other inmates. Only time would tell.

Lucas lay in his bed twisting and turning through the early evening until the bell rang signaling final roll call. He felt nauseous as he stood on the line outside his cell waiting for the count to be completed. As soon as the bell sounded, he backed into his cell and threw up in the metal toilette. Large beads of sweat dripped from his forehead, and he found it hard to crawl back to his bed.

Throughout the night Lucas continued to twist and turn, trying to find a position that didn't put pressure on his sore midsection. He had another bought of nausea at around midnight and threw up a second time. Getting sick again seemed to help, and Lucas slipped back into bed and closed his eyes.

A few minutes later, just before Lucas finally drifted off to sleep, the familiar image of Jim Powers' cold dead eyes appeared in his mind.

Rise and Shine

Lucas felt somewhat better the next morning. The pain in his side had dulled to a small ache, and he no longer felt nauseous when he stood up. He skipped his meal at breakfast, opting instead to just drink water and sip from a small glass of orange juice.

He looked around the mess hall, but didn't see any sign of Hector. He wondered how the young man had fared during his first night.

Entering the woodshop, Lucas wasted no time in getting everything setup. He had all the stations ready by the time the other prisoners started to arrive. He greeted each man and gave them their marching orders for the day.

It always surprised him by how well such hardened men took direction from a skinny old man. Working in the woodshop was considered a reward within the prison because it was one of Graybar's few air-conditioned workspaces. Plus, it beat the prison's other work areas, which consisted of backbreaking work stamping out license plates and road signs.

The crew had been hard at work for thirty minutes before Jerry led Hector through the shop entrance. Hector had a bandage round his right forearm and he was walking with a limp.

Jerry walked over to Lucas. "The fish got into a bit of a scuffle last night. He was caught alone in the bathroom after dinner and a couple Nazi punks tried to say hello. I told him he needs to make some friends soon. This is no place for loners."

Lucas just shook his head and motioned for Hector to get the sandpaper out of the cabinet.

"The warden is asking how things are looking for tomorrow," said Jerry.

"We should be fine. We have half the load ready now, and the rest should be mostly done by this afternoon. We may need to do some touch up work tomorrow morning, but not much."

"Sounds good Fosty. After that, you should get some rest. You are starting to look green around the gills old man."

"I will feel better after a couple nights of sleep."

With that Lucas walked over to Hector and pointed out a few areas that he needed to start sanding. "Finish smoothing out that box, and I'll show you how to apply the stain."

Hector didn't look up from his work. He just kept sanding away.

"You better start using your words fish!" grumbled Frank. "Have some respect for your elders."

Lucas smiled at Frank as he walked over to help him attach the hinges on a footlocker he was working on.

"Young punks don't have any damn respect anymore." The burly man glared at Hector.

"You are just getting old Frank," Lucas chuckled. "Besides, I think he is just afraid to say the wrong thing. I have seen some lost souls in this place, but he seems to be a little more lost than the others I have met."

"You aren't kidding there. That kid is in a tough spot. Even the Mexicans won't have anything to do with him. They don't have much use for Colombians. Too much cartel baggage. He is too brown to hang with the Nazi's and too light to hang with the brothers."

"Maybe the Holy Rollers will take him in?" Lucas offered.

"I doubt it. He doesn't seem like the preacher type, and even they don't know how to deal with drug runners."

Lucas wished he could help the young man, but he didn't know what could be done. Besides, his stomach had started to hurt again, and he still had plenty of work to get done before the end of the day.

Closing Time

By the end of the day, the crew had completed all thirty footlockers. The only thing left for Friday morning was to complete the final inspections and apply a final coat of varnish to each box.

The crew put away the tools and started filing out of the woodshop.

Lucas was relieved to be done for the day. His pain was worse now than it had been yesterday. Plus, the nausea was starting to return.

He called out to Jerry and asked if he could take a bathroom break.

The worried look on the guard's face told Lucas that he must look as bad as he felt. "Damn Fosty, your eyes are starting to turn yellow. We better get you over to see the doctor."

"That might be a good idea," Lucas grunted. "I just have to take a leak first."

Jerry waited outside the restroom as Lucas walked in and stepped up to the urinal. He felt another sharp pain in his side and took a deep breath. He gritted his teeth as he forced himself to pee. He felt a rush of relief as the stream started. He looked down to see that his urine was a bright crimson. A shudder coursed through his body, and he knew that something seriously was wrong.

He finished peeing, zipped up his pants and wiped away the sweat from his brow. He started to walk over to the sink just as a wave of nausea hit him. He made it to the trashcan just in time and threw up. His stomach was still empty, but somehow he managed to complete two violent puking sessions.

He stood back up and used a towel to wipe off his mouth. He was now very dizzy and had to use the sink to steady himself. He looked at himself in the mirror and could see that he was pale and sweating profusely. His eyes were a sickly yellow color, and he vision was starting to blur.

Lucas wasn't sure what to do. He tried to call out to Jerry, but he couldn't make his voice work. He steadied himself with the sink and tried to walk toward the door. He made it a few steps before his vision started to tunnel. He felt himself sinking to the floor and everything around him faded to black.

Bed Rest

All Lucas could see as he opened his eyes were blurry blobs. He could hear the voices of at least two medical personnel, one male and one female.

"Mister Fosterman, how are you feeling?" The male sounding blob asked.

"My head hurts."

"I'm sure it does," the voice intoned, which he could now see was coming from the prison doctor. "You hit your head on the bathroom floor. You have a mild contusion and probably a bit of a concussion."

"How long have I been out?"

"You came in about five hours ago; the guards wheeled you in on a gurney. Jerry said you haven't been feeling well for a few days, so I went ahead and drew some blood to start doing some tests. We can't do advanced testing here at the prison, but the results of a general blood test show that you have a very low white blood cell count. Your eyes are also jaundiced."

"It all started with my stomach, which still hurts like hell."

"Here on the right side?" The doctor came around to take a look. He pressed a few times and watched Lucas' face to see what areas elicited the most pain. The doctor didn't look much older than thirty. He wore a military-style buzzcut and thick horn-rimmed glasses.

"Well, you definitely have something going on with one of your organs. I am going to draw some more blood and send it out to a local lab. We should know more in a day or two, but for now you are restricted to bed. We are going to leave the catheter in, but Zoe here will take the breathing tube out."

Lucas laid his head back as the nurse came over and started unhooking his breathing tube. She was a heavy-set lady with short cropped brown hair and tattoos running up both arms. As she stood over him pulling out the tube, he could see that she had a bull ring hanging from her nose.

Fortuitous Roommates

Lucas was wheeled into a room in the prison's intensive care unit where an orderly helped Zoe move him from his ER gurney to a hospital bed. As he was being shuffled around he could see that he wasn't the only prisoner in the room. There was another occupied bed, but he couldn't see the other patient.

Once he was in position, the nurse hooked up his IV and repositioned his catheter tube and bag. She then used a syringe to pump some medicine into his IV and walked out of the room.

He waited until the nurse and orderly had left before lifting his head to checkout his roommate. He was surprised to see Hector laying in the bed. His face was bruised and swollen and he had a large bandage wrapped around his midsection. He had obviously been beaten by someone, or more likely, by a few people.

Lucas lay back down and shook his head. He could probably guess what had happened to the young man. After a while he closed his eyes and let the drugs carry him off to sleep.

He was awoken a while later when he heard the doctor talking to Hector.

"The swelling around your eyes and nose should go down in a couple of days. I did what I could to reset your broken nose, but we'll have to see how it looks after the swelling subsides."

The tall doctor pulled back the bandages surrounding his abdomen and adjusted his glasses for a better look. "You have a lacerated liver and a good amount of internal bleeding. We will continue to take blood every four hours until we are sure that the bleeding has stopped. Then you are going to have to lay still for the next few days."

"Thank you doctor." Hector's voice was weak.

"And how are you doing, Mister Fosterman." The doctor sounded casual.

"I am doing just fine now that my stomach has stopped hurting so much." Lucas pushed the button to lift the front of his bed up.

"I'm sure the morphine has something to do with that," said the doctor as he inspected Lucas' head. "It looks like you guys are going to be roommates for a week or so. I expect both of you to stay in bed and get as much rest as possible."

With that the doctor walked out of the room, leaving the two men sitting in uncomfortable silence. Eventually, Lucas broke the tension. "Well, they do not have a clue what is going on with me. Something about a bad organ and jaundice. I have to lay here for three days until a blood test comes back."

"Apparently, I am allergic to the fists of large white supremacists." Hector let out a little chuckle.

Both men laughed a bit and Hector started talking about what had landed him in the infirmary.

Turns out a couple lonely muscle heads had taken a liking to Hector's youthful figure and cornered him in the shower. Most newbies would have just let nature take its course, but Hector fought them off with everything he had. He had cracked one of the large men in the nose, which escalated things from attempted rape to assault and battery. The two men punched and kicked him until he was a bloody mess.

Lucas was proud of the young man for standing his ground, and he hoped it would be enough to prove to the other inmates that he was not as weak as he first appeared.

The two men spent the next two weeks together in the hospital room getting to know each other.

Lucas shared his story about how he had been sentenced to life in prison for killing the man who had raped and murdered his precious little Katie. He talked about all the reasons he felt it was necessary to give relief to his family. He also talked about how the guilt never went away. About how he saw Jim Power's face every time he closed his eyes. About how he feared he would never get to see his wife Sarah and precious little Katie in heaven. About how he had spent every day in Graybar trying to atone for his sins.

It didn't take Hector long to improve his English as he told Lucas about life back in Colombia. Lucas was enthralled listening to Hector talk about his childhood in the cartel work camp and his time serving as a driver. He was shocked listening to his story about being selected to run a shipment of drugs from Colombia to Louisiana. He was heartbroken when he saw Hector cry as he talked about what had likely happened to his mother and father.

The part that struck Lucas the hardest was when Hector talked about his younger brother Miguel. Hector knew there was no hope for his older brother, Juan, who had embraced and even enjoyed life in the cartel. But there had still been hope for young Miguel.

As the days progressed, Lucas listened intently to Hector's stories. He made mental notes of every name, date, and place. He didn't know why it was so important to hold on to those details, but something in his gut told him that his world was about to change.

Misguided Atonement

"Fools base their thoughts on foolish assumptions, so their conclusions will be wicked madness."

— Ecclesiastes 10:13

Summer 2016

A Rude Awakening

Rudy Romero started to wake up. His head felt like it weighed a ton. There was a metallic taste in his mouth, along with gritty sand. He opened his eyes. The sunlight was blinding. It was obvious he was outside, but he would have to wait for his eyes to adjust before knowing more.

It was hot... very hot. He sat up and shook his head trying to clear away the haze. That's when he felt a raw spot where a collar was digging into his neck. He pulled at the collar and tried to find a way to take it off. There was no buckle or latch that he could feel.

His vision began to clear a bit and he could tell that he was under a white canopy of some sort. He was pretty certain he wasn't in San Diego anymore. He was in the desert. And he was alone.

Next to him was a wooden folding chair. He grabbed the seat and tried to stand up. He made it to his feet but immediately slumping into the chair. He was very dizzy. His head was pounding.

He held his hands to his head and squeezed his eyes shut trying to steady himself. When he opened his eyes again he began to take better stock of his surroundings. To his left was a large green cooler. To his right was a six-foot folding table that held what looked like a rifle case. There was also a scope of some sort, a pair of earmuffs and a walkie-talkie.

Just outside the canopy he could see yellow police tape surrounding the perimeter. He could also see signs adorned with large skulls and crossbones, lightning bolts and the words "Do Not Cross." He grabbed the collar around his neck and started to get the idea just how dire his situation might be.

He tried standing up again and was more successful this

time. He was still unsteady, so he placed his hands on the folding table for support. He began surveying the horizon trying to figure out where was. As he looked out in every direction all he could see was never-ending desert, sand dunes, a few cacti, and lots of dry shrubs. The only obstacle he noticed was a white rectangular panel sitting what seemed like a mile away. It had three black dots on the front.

It took him a couple more minutes before he felt comfortable walking around. He was insanely thirsty, so he decided to investigate the cooler first. He could see thick condensation on the sides, so he knew it was cold inside. He gently moved the latch aside and grabbed the lid with a firm hand. He threw the lid open jumping back as a cautionary move. He was relieved to see that the cooler was filled with several water bottles and an assortment of meats, cheeses, fruit, and other foods.

He grabbed a bottle of water from the cooler and looked it over. Seeing that the seal was still intact, he opened the bottle and guzzled the contents. He grabbed a second bottle of water and closed the lid.

He walked over to the table. Upon closer inspection, he could see that the scope was a spotting scope used by long-range rifle shooters. He took off the cap and used the scope to spy the white panel he had seen earlier.

He could now see that the panel looked like a small target range. The three black dots were actually target silhouettes, simulating the head and shoulders of a man laying prone. The panel itself looked like it was made out of metal. About one hundred yards from the panel he could see a green range flag sitting on top of a metal pole. The wind was blowing lightly, and he could tell by the flag's position that the wind speed was about five miles an hour. He stood back up and furrowed his brow in confusion.

Next he looked at the large black case. It was a Pelican hard case, and it looked new. He opened the six latches sealing it and flipped open the lid. He immediately recognized the contents. It was a Barrett 98b sniper rifle with a Harris bipod. He would know that model anywhere. He owned three and had spent hours on his private range shooting similar rifles. He also recognized the Nightforce scope, which was his preferred brand of optics. The whole setup could have been taken directly from his personal stock.

Looking through the case, he also found a box of twenty .338 Lapua Magnum rounds, a digital temperature gauge, and two empty magazines. Not knowing what to expect, he wasted no time in pulling out the rifle. He set up the bipod and placed the rifle in front of him on the table. He then loaded the magazines with ten rounds each. He stuffed one magazine in his pocket and inserted the other into the rifle. He slid the bolt home, chambering a round.

He immediately felt more at ease knowing that he was now armed. And armed with a weapon he was very comfortable using. He had killed at least six men with rifles using this configuration.

He pulled the chair up to the table and took a seat directly behind the rifle. He looked through the scope and pointed the weapon at the white target panel. Once he was comfortably sighted in, he decided it was time to see what this was all about.

He picked up the walkie-talkie and pressed the transmit button. "Hello."

A response came a few seconds later.

"Hello Mister Romero. My name is Lucas Fosterman. I believe we are both in for a very exciting afternoon."

Four Months Earlier

One Last Night

Lucas reread the same page for a third time before setting his book down. He couldn't concentrate. He still couldn't believe he was going home tomorrow.

For the past ten years he had been living in the geriatric wing of the Graybar Penitentiary. After being diagnosed with pancreatic cancer several months ago, he had expected to spend his remaining days in Cell Block D. But fate had other plans.

The last six months had been especially rough. After a battery of tests, the doctors had informed him that he only had about a year to live. He had spent several weeks in the infirmary, and he was no longer well enough to work in the woodshop. Instead, he spent time in the library helping some of the younger inmates earn their GED's and other education certificates. He hated not being able to work with his hands, but he at least felt like he was still doing some good.

Eventually, all the good deeds he had done in Graybar over the past ten years had led to a rare recommendation by Warden Buckman. The warden had personally put in a request for Lucas to be released under the state's newly-authorized compassionate release program.

Three months later Lucas received a letter from the state parole board stating that he was under consideration for compassionate release. He was shocked; especially since he had no idea the warden had even submitted the request.

Lucas still had to go through several steps before the final approval was given. He had to prove that his illness was terminal, which was easy enough to verify with prison medical records.

He also had to prove that he had a place to live and family who could help care for him. That was the easiest step of all. His sons were elated when they heard the news that their dad could possibly be released. Both men wrote enthusiastic letters stating they were ready and willing to accept their father into their homes. Mark went overboard sending pictures of his guest room complete with a new hospital bed and baby monitors.

The approval for release was made official late on Friday. The warden had delivered the news in person, telling Lucas that he would be going home on Monday. Lucas was even allowed to use the warden's cell phone to call Mark and deliver the good news.

The prison bell rang, signaling Sunday free time. Lucas rolled out of his bunk, headed out of his cell, and walked down the hallway to the prison chapel. Sunday morning church service started at 9 am and he wanted to be there early to say goodbye to a young man he had been mentoring over the past few months.

He got to the chapel at a little past 8:30. He sat down in his usual seat and smiled when he saw Hector Morales walk into the room.

Most people would have written Hector off as just another criminal. A typical drug stooge who was trying to make money peddling poison to the masses. Lucas had spent a lot of time with Hector over the past several months and knew that nothing could have been further from the truth.

Hector was excited when he heard the news that his fiend was going to be released, and he was happy they would get to spend one last Sunday together. The two men spent the day talking about the future.

Hector was still filled with sadness about his family. He hadn't received any word from Colombia since arriving at the prison, and he doubted that any of his remaining family members even knew that he was in Graybar – If any of his family was still alive.

Lucas tried to comfort Hector the best he could, but he knew there was no use. It was likely that his mother and father were gone now, and there was no telling what had happened to his two brothers.

The next day Lucas started going through the paces of the prison's lengthy release process. He spent over an hour dealing with the legal and parole departments, even longer reviewing his medical records and getting releases and instructions for all his daily medications.

By the time he completed his final sign offs, it was almost 4 pm when then guard took him to his last stop at the warden's office. Warden Buckman stayed behind his desk and gave Lucas a stern talk about making good decisions and becoming a productive member of his community and family for the short time he had left on this Earth. Once the lecture was over, the warden stood up, shook Lucas' hand, and smiled. "Thank you for making such a positive difference in this place, and I hope to never see you come back again."

Finally, Lucas was allowed to use the phone to call Mark and let him know that he would be ready to be picked up by 4:30. His anxious sons were already waiting for him in the lot.

Lucas was led back to Cell Block D and the gray cell he had called home for the past ten years. There he picked up the small box holding his belongings and followed the guard back toward the exit.

As he walked past the other prisoners he was offered a few goodbyes from some of the old timers. The well-wishes got louder as they moved from the geriatric ward to the main population hall. As they got close to the exit, he stopped for a second at Hector's cell.

"Don't worry son," Lucas smiled at his friend. "I promise you will leave this prison someday and find a better life."

Welcome Home

Lucas stepped out of the prison door and into the bright afternoon sunlight. His sons waved at him from outside the prison gate. They had been waiting for their dad for more than three hours, wanting to get him away from the awful place as quickly as possible.

They gave each other long hugs, and Mark teared up just a bit. Paul made sure his dad sat shotgun and climbed into the back of Mark's new red Ford F-250 work truck. The graphics on the side read "Fosterman Custom Furniture," which made Lucas smile with pride.

"Business must be good if you can afford a truck like this." Lucas smiled while looking around the cab of the new truck.

"Paul has one too," said Mark. "We got them last month, along with a new delivery truck. I guess I forgot to tell you about all that with everything that's been going on the past few weeks. I can't wait for you to see the showroom."

Lucas was happy to know that business was going well for the boys. He had gifted them 50/50 ownership in the custom furniture store about twelve years ago, and they had worked hard to build it into a strong family business. Over the past ten years, Mark and Paul had passed the time during their monthly prison visits going over the changes with the business. They even brought along financial reports from time to time to show how good things were going.

The drive home was filled with excited talk about the business and the latest events with the family. Lucas tried to keep up, but he was having a hard time staying focused. He had lived life at a slow shuffle over the past ten years, and he needed to acclimate to the fast pace of the outside world.

As they pulled into Mark's driveway, he was thrilled at the sight of his old Chevy pickup truck sitting in the driveway. The old girl was over fifty years old at this point, but she still looked good.

Seeing the surprise on his dad's face, Paul leaned up from the backseat. "Doesn't it look great? We kept it in storage this whole time. We took it out last month and went through everything. We made sure the motor was tip top, replaced the tires, filters, belts, everything. It's as good as new."

"I thought for sure you guys would have dumped the old goat by now." Lucas laughed.

"We didn't have the heart to sell it. We just kept it stored away at the workshop. We took it out on drives every few months. And every Memorial Day we took it to Mom and Katie's grave sites," Mark interjected, his voice trailing a bit when he mentioned Katie.

Just then, the front door burst open and out ran Paul's wife Debbie, Lucas' brother Steve, and his sister Tammy. They all ran up and hugged Lucas.

A few seconds later, Mark's wife Lisa walked out the door. She walked up to Lucas tears already welling up in her eyes. She wrapped her arms around him and buried her head in his chest. She didn't even try to hold back the tears and started to sob.

Lucas knew she wasn't crying tears of sorrow, but they weren't really tears of joy either. He just hugged her back as tight as he could and cried along with her, letting the memories and emotions of the past several years wash over them.

After Jim's murder and Lucas' plea bargain for a life sentence, the family had no choice but to begin to come to terms with Katie's death and move on with life. His sons went back to work building the furniture business. Mark and Lisa's son Tyler went to college and was eventually commissioned as an officer in the Marine Corps. Paul and Debbie used their vacation time and some newfound wealth thanks to a gift from Lucas to travel around the world. Best of all, Mark and Lisa got back together and remarried just after Tyler's graduation from the University of Maryland.

After almost five minutes, Lisa let go of her hold on Lucas and started wiping away the tears. Lucas also used his sleeve to wipe away some tears and looked around to see that everyone else had also been crying.

"So how is my grandson?" Lucas asked, trying to break the tension.

Lisa smiled. "He is flying in later tonight. And he is bringing another new girlfriend."

Back to the Real World

Four weeks after Lucas was released from prison, he still hadn't fully adjusted to life outside of his cell. But he knew he didn't have much time to get things together. For a seventy-six-year-old man with stage four pancreatic cancer, he felt surprisingly strong. Still, he knew his health wouldn't hold out for much longer.

He had spent most of the past three weeks visiting with various family members and friends. He loved being able to drive his old truck into town to spend time with his sons at the furniture showroom. He had been amazed by how big it had grown over the past decade; taking up nearly half a city block now. They had four sales reps working at the showroom and more than a dozen craftsmen in the workshop. When he had given the showroom to the boys it was half the size and employed only six people.

Lucas would get up early to spend time working in the workshop while it was still cool. He would usually head into the showroom at around 11 am to spend an hour or so with his sons before heading to lunch at the Daily Diner.

In the afternoons, Lucas would retreat to the old farmhouse that used to belong to his mother. The property now belonged to Mark, and it was a few miles out of town in a remote area of farm country. The farmhouse was rundown, but the cellar next to the house had been kept in good shape.

The family now used the cellar as a storage room to hold canned goods, antique tools, and a large gun safe where they stored their favorite deer rifles and other assorted weapons.

Behind the farmhouse was a large field that opened up to nearly two miles of cleared land before ending at a thick tree line. The farmhouse was situated in the center of the property, which totaled just over seventy acres, making the area around the house completely private.

In the middle of the open field sat a variety of metal gong targets with large orange signs sitting on top marking the yardages. There were nine targets in total marking distances of 300 yards, 500 yards, 750 yards, 1,000 yards, 1,500 yards, and one mile. Each target was made of a two-foot square piece of heavy steel plate that had been painted bright green with a six-inch red dot in the center.

On this warm sunny day in August, Lucas arrived at the farmhouse at around 3 pm, which was his normal arrival time. He had been to the farmhouse every afternoon for the past month, and he was glad to see that the sun was shining brightly without a cloud in the sky.

He went down into the cellar, walked up to the large gun safe, and dialed the combination into the lock. He opened the large door and pulled out a stainless steel rifle case and a small shooting bag. He turned and walked back out of the cellar, grabbing a rolled up shooting mat on his way up the stairs.

Just past the cellar door sat a wood picnic table that was covered by a canvas canopy. The canopy extended about ten feet past the table allowing plenty of room for him to unroll the shooting mat and keep it fully situated in the shade.

He walked back to the table and opened the stainless steel case revealing a desert tan sniper rifle.

The rifle was a Surgeon Remedy 1581 XL Action rifle made by the Surgeon Rifles company. It was chambered in .338 Lapua Magnum and featured a Cadex Dual Strike stock complete with Harris bipod and a heavy match-grade twenty-seven inch barrel. The trigger pull had been reduced to 1.75 pounds, which was about the best his shaky old hands could handle. The rifle was topped by a U.S. Optics ER-25 5-25X scope. This magnificent scope was rated for sighting in targets more than 2,000 yards away, but he had never taken it out quite that far.

He opened the small shooting bag and pulled out a twenty count box of .338 Lapua Magnum rounds and four, five-round magazines. He also pulled out a pair of Swarovski range-finding binoculars. He had always preferred using binoculars over spotting scopes.

He loaded the four magazines with five rounds each and placed one magazine in the rifle, but left the bolt locked to the rear. He gently set the rifle on the shooting mat facing down range and placed the three extra magazines to the right edge of the mat. He uncapped the binoculars and set them on the left edge of the mat.

Lucas then stood straight up, closed his eyes, and took two deep breaths to steady himself. He began going through his regular routine of stretches. Placing his hands behind his head and twisting first to the left, then to the right. Next, he bent down and touched his toes followed by a few squats and a couple of deep knee bends to each side.

Once he felt properly limbered up, he faced down range looking at the most distant targets. He placed his feet at the edge of the shooting mat and closed his eyes again. He took a full two minutes visualizing what he needed to do. Once ready, he lifted his wrist watch and started the timer.

He quickly dropped to the mat and configured his body in a prone position behind the rifle. He took a quick glance at the range flag seeing that the wind was blowing at about ten miles an hour. He made a few adjustments to the scope before firmly pushing the bolt forward, chambering a round. He clicked off the safety and pointed the rifle at the 1,500-yard gong. He took a few deep breaths, then exhaling he squeezed the trigger. There was a short delay, then he heard the sound of the gong.

He picked up the binoculars and looked at the target to see where the round had hit. He was ten inches to the right and eight inches high of the red dot in the center. He made a couple of adjustments to the scope and settled back behind the rifle to repeat the process.

He took four more shots at the 1,500-yard line before he had to change magazines. He was growing frustrated because he still hadn't hit the red dot even once. Two shots had been high and to the right, one shot had been pulled completely off target. At least the last shot was just an inch from the red.

He fired three more shots. This time all three landed in the red. Now he was ready to move on to the one-mile target.

He readjusted his body slightly to sight in on the one-mile target. Even though the target was only 260 yards further down range, it was much harder for his old eyes to bring into focus. He took two deep breathes, then exhaled before squeezing the trigger. He heard the crack of the rifle as his ninth round flew down range. He waited for the delay, then nothing. Damn, he missed.

He cycled the bolt and tried again. The tenth round went down range. Again, nothing. Frustrated, he ejected the magazine and inserted a fresh one.

He decided to go back to the 1,500-yard target to recalibrate himself. He shot three more rounds, all of which landed in the red. He was happy with those results, and returned to the one-mile target.

He took a bit more time to steady himself and focused in on the blurry target. He took two breaths, exhaled and squeezed the trigger. He waited for the delay, then he heard the ring of the gong.

He decided not to pick up the binoculars to see where the round hit, instead he cycled the bolt and sited in again. Two breaths, exhale, squeeze, delay… a second bong sound.

He quickly stopped his watch and reviewed the time: 8 minutes 44 seconds. Still not a great time, he told himself, but it was the best time he had posted to date.

When he first started his training three weeks ago, he couldn't even hit the 1,000-yard target with any regularity. It took him a week before he felt ready to move up to 1,500 yards. After two weeks, he started making attempt at the one-mile target. For the past five days, he had hit the target at least once each time before running through the allotted twenty rounds.

Finished with his routine, he packed up the shooting mat, bag, and rifle. He returned everything to the safe in the cellar, grabbed a can of green spray paint, and headed out to the targets.

The long walk out to the one-mile target always solidified the fact that it was a ridiculously-long distance to shoot a rifle. As a young man, it had taken years for him to get moderately proficient at this distance, but he was far from a young man now. And he was sorely out of practice.

He reached the one-mile target and looked at the white and black spider-shaped marks made by the bullets. One mark was five inches to the left and seven inches low. The other was three inches to the right and four inches high. He nodded his head in approval before clearing the marks with green paint.

Next, he backtracked to the 1,500-yard target and shook his head at the grouping. Many target shooters would be very pleased to place eleven rounds within a one-foot grouping at 1,500 yards. But this wasn't about target shooting. This was about life and death.

Final Preparations

It had now been a full two months since Lucas had been released from prison. He had used every ounce of that time spending his days with family and friends, his afternoons at the farmhouse, and his evenings making preparations. He had originally been grateful to have two months to prepare before carrying out the final phase of his plan. However, a visit to the hospital a couple weeks ago to review the status of his cancer markers had given him cause for alarm.

His oncologist had regurgitated a string of medical gobbledygook, but it all boiled down to the fact that he was starting to die. And it was going to start getting bad sooner than later. The doctor's best guess was that his body would start shutting down in about a month, possibly even within a couple weeks. Lucas knew he had to do his best to keep himself in shape before it got to that point if he was going to even have a chance at completing his mission.

Now it was the day before he planned to leave, and all the preparations had been made. His truck was parked in its usual spot in Mark's garage. He had recently purchased a custom, lockable tonneau cover for his truck bed, which was already filled to the brim with all the supplies he needed. He reviewed the contents one last time before securing the tonneau cover. Once he was confident that everything was ready, he closed the garage door and headed into the house.

It was Friday evening, and he had made plans to go to dinner with Mark and Paul. The three men spent the evening eating steaks at their favorite restaurant and talked about many of the good times they had experienced together. Lucas was very pleased that the evening had gone so well. He knew he couldn't tell them anything about his plans, so this dinner would have to serve as a final goodbye.

He told the boys he planned to leave the next morning for a three-day trip to Branson, Missouri to see some old friends. The boys knew the friends he was talking about, so they had no reason to doubt his intentions. He hated lying to them, but he knew it was for the best.

Before Paul left, Lucas gave him a big hug and told him he loved him. He also hugged Mark goodnight and told him he was all packed up and planned to leave early the next morning before the sun came up to avoid traffic. Lucas headed off to the bathroom to take a shower and get ready for bed. He laid down in the bed ready for sleep. He looked over at the clock, which read 10:14. Even ten years ago he would have been too nervous and excited to sleep at a time like this. Now he was too old and too tired to worry about tomorrow. He closed his eyes and quickly drifted off to sleep.

He woke up the next morning at a little past 5:30 am. He spent less than fifteen minutes in the bathroom getting ready before jumping in his truck. He backed out of the garage pausing at the end of the long driveway. He looked at Mark's house one last time, saying a silent goodbye to his family.

He then headed southwest on Interstate 44, but he didn't

make the turn toward Branson as he had told his boys he planned to do. Instead, he continued west.

Damn the Heat

It was early Sunday afternoon by the time he rolled into Yuma, Arizona. He stopped at a gas station to fuel up and refill two large coolers with a mix of dry and cubed ice. Then he continued westward out of town for a few miles before turning north at the sand dunes.

He drove through the desert hardscape for nearly forty-five minutes in uninhabited territory. He was familiar with this area from his time in the Marine Corps, but it had been more than fifty years since he had traveled this way. Satellite images on Google showed that the area remained barren and untouched, and he was surprised at how much he still recognized of the desert terrain.

A ping on his hand-held GPS unit confirmed that he had reached his destination. He looked around his surroundings seeing nothing but desert, sand dunes, cacti, and a few shrubs in every direction. He pulled his truck up to the first GPS waypoint, making sure he parked directly over the blinking dot.

As he opened his truck door, the heat rushed in with a blast. It was just past 5 pm and the temperature was well above 100 degrees. Probably closer to 110 degrees. He grabbed a straw hat from the cab and stuffed a sweat towel into his pocket. He was going to need it.

He unlocked the tonneau cover and started pulling out supplies for the first location. He started with a twelve-foot by twelve-foot white pop-up shade canopy, which helped to reduce the heat and provided relief from the blinding sunlight. Next, he pulled out a six-foot white plastic folding table and a wooden folding chair and set them up in the middle of the canopy.

His arm and back muscles strained as he took out a heavy

green cooler and let it slam on the ground. He dragged it the remainder of the way to its final resting place. He opened the cooler to check the contents. Along with the large block of dry ice and ice cubes was a number of water bottles, some fruit, cheeses, meat sticks, and other assorted snack foods. Nothing fancy.

Then he pulled out a large black gun case, spotting scope, shooting mat, earmuffs, and digital temperature gauge and positioned them on the table. He turned on the temperature gauge and it soon read 108 degrees. He rolled the shooting mat out in front of the table so that it laid just inside the shade of the canopy.

The hardest part came when he ventured out from under the cover of the canopy to run a wire for an invisible fence. He used a metal poker to push the wire into the ground, positioning the fence about two feet out from the perimeter of the canopy. It took him almost an hour to get the fencing settled into the ground before hooking up the electrical leads to a portable generator. He also placed some wood stakes in the ground and ran yellow police tape around the perimeter. Finally, he planted a couple of signs showing big skulls and crossbones, lightning bolts and the words "Do Not Cross."

He checked the gas in the generator to make sure it was completely full before slipping a heavy metal cover over it and ducking back under the canopy. He sat in the wood chair for a few minutes wiping away the sweat from his brow. He stole a bottle of water from the cooler and downed it in a couple of long pulls. Damn the heat. And damn his old body.

He made a few last-minute adjustments to the equipment before jumping back in his truck. He grabbed the hand-held GPS and made sure he was still positioned on top of the first waypoint. He scrolled the GPS screen out so that he could see a second waypoint directly in front of his position. He then zeroed out his truck's trip odometer. He started driving slowly toward the second waypoint, watching both the odometer and GPS as the distance increased. Once he was almost directly over the waypoint, he switched to monitoring only the odometer waiting for it to roll from .9 miles to directly over the 1.0-mile mark.

Arriving at the second location, he unloaded similar equipment as he had placed under the first canopy. He started with the twelve-foot by twelve-foot white pop-up canopy, folding table, wooden chair, large green cooler, temperature gauge, shooting mat, and earmuffs.

He also unloaded a stainless-steel gun case holding his Surgeon Remedy 1581 XL Action rifle and took out his Swarovski range-finding binoculars. He looked through the binoculars toward the first location and was pleased to see that the rangefinder showed the location to be exactly one mile away. He was also pleased to see that he had a clear line of site to the canopy with no sand dunes or cacti in the way.

Once he was sure that all the equipment was setup to his satisfaction, he climbed back in the truck and pulled it around so that the bed was lined up directly in front of the canopy. He only had one shot to get this right.

He jumped out of the truck and made sure that he was positioned correctly. Not satisfied, he jumped back in and repositioned the truck closer to the canopy. Next, he opened the tailgate and rolled out a heavy five-gallon bucket filled with concrete and a pole sticking out from the middle. He rolled the bucket out to the side and returned for a second pole holding a green flag. He carried the second pole to the bucket and slid it over the first pole to complete the portable range flag.

Now the only thing sitting in the truck bed was a large white panel that covered the entire bed. He grabbed the end of the panel and started pulling it. The panel was sitting on a series of small plastic pipes, which allowed it to easily roll out of the bed. He gave it a hard yank as it cleared the truck bed and plopped down in the sand. He gave it a few hard kicks to make sure it was parallel to the front of the canopy. It took everything he had to stand up the heavy wood and steel panel so that it covered the entire front area of the canopy. He lowered four hinged 2x4 braces that now held the panel in place.

He stepped back in front of the panel, giving him the same view he would see from the first location. From this vantage point all you could see was the large white panel with three target silhouettes. The black silhouettes looked huge from this position, but he knew they would look like small black dots from a mile away.

He had to take one final break and down a second bottle of water before rolling the portable range flag out about 200 yards from the second position. He had originally planned to place it halfway between the two canopies, but he was starting to feel weak and lightheaded.

By the time he made it back to the truck, he was dizzy and almost passed out as he grabbed the door handle. He was thankful to be back in the air-conditioned cab and laid his arms across the steering wheel and set his head down for a few minutes. He took a few deep breaths and noticed that blood had started leaking out of his nose. He wiped it away with a rag, but that didn't stop the flow. He grabbed another bottle of water from his small truck cooler and placed it behind his head. He put the rag over his nose and squeezed it. He closed his eyes for a while waiting for the bleeding to stop. This was his third nose bleed of the day. He really hated having cancer.

The Shady Chauffeur

Lucas was now at the Hotel Del Coronado; his favorite hotel in San Diego. He and Sarah had spent their honeymoon at this hotel, and it had always been one of his favorite places.

He had arrived at the hotel last night at a little after 10 pm. He had gone straight to his room and plopped down on his bed. He didn't even have time to get undressed or take his boots off before passing out from exhaustion. Luckily his internal alarm clock woke him up at 5 am, leaving him plenty of time to make final preparations.

He called the rental car service to confirm that his town car had been delivered to the hotel yesterday afternoon. He was told that the car was in the self-parking lot and the keys had been left with the desk clerk as instructed.

Next, he called room service and ordered breakfast along with two extra cups of French Roast coffee and some extra bottles of water. Then he jumped in the shower to wash away the sand and sweat. He barely had time to finish putting on his black three-piece suit and tie before room service arrived.

He ate his breakfast on the balcony of his room watching the waves of the Pacific Ocean roll in. He wished he had time to take one last stroll down the beach to look at all the Navy vessels and other ships cruising the harbor. But time was no longer his friend.

He quickly brushed his teeth and stuffed his dirty clothes into a duffel bag. He then grabbed a drink holder and filled it with the two cups of coffee and two bottles of water. He grabbed a sealed letter addressed to his son Mark. He also grabbed a FedEx envelope, opened it, inserted the sealed letter, and threw in his truck keys. Before leaving the room, he sealed the envelope and addressed it to Mark's house in Missouri.

In the lobby, he walked up to the counter and handed the FedEx envelope to the desk clerk and asked him to include it in their daily mail run. He also asked the clerk for the keys that the car service had left for him.

He exited the back of the hotel leading to the self-parking lot and headed to the back of the lot. Stopping at his old truck, he threw the duffle bag in the back of the bed. He patted the truck and nodded his head goodbye before turning to enter the back of a black Lincoln Town Car parked a few spots down. He placed one of the cups of coffee and a water bottle into the car's drink caddy. He looked over the backseat to make sure there were no obvious signs that the vehicle was a rental. He then jumped into the driver's seat and adjusted the side mirrors and pointed the rearview mirror so that he could clearly see the backseat. He stuffed the rental paperwork in the center console and looked over the interior of the car one last time. Everything was set.

He slipped on a chauffeur's hat and headed out of the parking lot.

He drove about half a mile down the island before arriving at the Hotel Marisol. He pulled into the waiting area and told the valet that he was there to pick up Mister Romero. The valet ran inside and came out about three minutes later ushering a tall dark haired man to the Town Car. Lucas recognized the man from pictures he had seen on internet searches and knew he was definitely Rudy Romero.

Getting in, the man offered a grumbled hello before turning his attention back to a call on his cell phone. "Tell them, I will be back in three days. I have business to finish here, and I will take care of their problems when I get back. You just make sure that everything stays on track. We can't afford any more problems. I don't want excuses, just do your job."

"Good morning Mister Romero. We are right on time for your appointment," Lucas locked eyes with his passenger through the rearview mirror. "If you would like coffee or water, there are fresh cups in the holders in front of you."

"What?" The Colombian replied absently. "Oh. Yes, yes. Thank You."

Rudy Romero continued fussing with his cell phone firing off texts and reviewing emails.

Lucas became nervous as he eyed the man through the mirror. He wondered if he was ever going to drink his coffee or water. He knew he liked French Roast coffee.

A few minutes later, Mister Romero put his phone down and grabbed the cup of coffee. "How long is the drive?" he asked before taking a drink.

"It will only be a few minutes, sir. We just have to cross the bridge and drive a few miles from there." Lucas watched him take a few more drinks of his coffee.

"This is French Roast, no. Very good. I like this."

"Yes, sir. I have more if you want."

"No, I shouldn't drink so much before my surgery."

As they crossed the Coronado Bridge, Lucas continued taking short glances into his mirror. He watched as Rudy Romero put his cell phone down and rubbed his eyes. He saw the man shake his head and look around dazed. Eventually, Mister Romero made eye contact with Lucas through the mirror. The man looked confused, then knowing, then angry. But it was too late. Before he could say anything his head tilted sideways and he slumped over in the back seat, fast asleep.

The Long Hot Wait

Lucas sat on the wooden folding chair under the shade of his canopy. His nose was bleeding again. He was having trouble slowing his heart rate and controlling his breathing. It had taken all his strength to drag the bulky drug lord out of the back seat of the town car and under the canopy.

He was starting to have doubts that he could pull this off. What was he thinking? He was a seventy-six-year-old man, with stage four cancer. He was in okay shape for such an old man, but the cancer had progressed quickly over the past few days and his body was starting to breakdown. It was too late to worry about any of that now.

It was just after 11:30 am, and he knew that he didn't have much time. Rudy Romero would be waking up soon. He needed to get himself together. He grabbed a water bottle from his cooler, placed it behind his neck, and laid his head down on the table. He closed his eyes and tried to calm down. He started to think back about the series of events that had led him down this path.

In prison, Hector Morales didn't have many happy stories, but they were still intriguing. He talked about working the fields as a young man and how he sang songs to entertain himself. He talked about how hard life was for his parents and brothers. He talked about working at the garage and docks. He talked about becoming a driver and learning English. He talked about all the gossip he learned while shuttling Mariana throughout Colombia.

Lucas was especially interested in all the gossip Hector had heard over the years. Hector talked all about the Romero's preferences and daily schedules. He described Rudy's private shooting range and the types of weapons he liked to use. Hector laughed when he talked about Rudy's erectile issues and his ugly birthmark. Hector even mentioned that Rudy had an appointment in San Diego in a few months to have cosmetic surgery to have the birthmark removed. Hector remembered the date because it was the same day as his mother's birthday. Hector talked about how secretive Mariana had been about the surgery because other men in the cartel would not understand how Rudy could be so vain as to have cosmetic surgery. Not even Rudy's most trusted advisors knew that he was scheduled for such a "feminine" operation.

Once Lucas heard about that appointment, he knew it was a once in a lifetime opportunity. He just had to figure out a way to capitalize on it.

"Hello." The sound of Rudy Romero coming through the walkie-talkie jolted Lucas from his daydream. He wiped his nose and saw that the bleeding had stopped. He sat back in the seat and took a deep breath.

Let the adventure begin.

The Setup

"Hello Mister Romero. My name is Lucas Fosterman. I believe we are both in for a very exciting afternoon."

"Who the hell are you? I don't know any Lucas Fosterman." He recognized the voice as the old man who had picked him up this morning. Now he was even more confused.

"Listen closely, Mister Romero. It is currently 11:43. At exactly noon, the white panel you see in the distance will come down. At that point, I will start shooting at you. The distance between us is exactly one mile. We both have custom rifles chambered in .338 Lapua Magnum. We both have our preferred optics. We both have exactly twenty rounds of ammunition. Just before noon, I will call the California Highway Patrol and give them our GPS coordinates. It will take them at least forty-five minutes to arrive at this location. You may take as many practice shots as you wish, but remember you only have twenty rounds. Do you understand, Mister Romero?"

There was a pause before the reply. "I understand. But I want you to know Lucas Fosterman that I am going to kill you today. Then I am going to kill your family and everyone you love. Now do you understand me, Lucas Fosterman?"

A wave of shock hit Lucas. In all his planning, he never considered that his family would be threatened. This had always been his solo mission. He felt his heart start racing again and his blood pressure skyrocketed. A knot started to well up in his stomach and he felt like he was about to throw up.

"Yes, Mister Romero. I understand," Lucas replied through gritted teeth. "By the Grace of God, may the best man live."

With that, Lucas turned off the two-way radio.

He sat in in his chair in numb silence for a few minutes waiting to see how the cartel leader would react. There was a chance that Rudy would simply build a bunker out of the table and cooler and hide behind them until the authorities arrived. Lucas knew that option was highly unlikely given the drug lord's violent nature and overbearing machismo. Still, all he could do now was wait.

Focus the Rage

Rudy Romero had listened to Lucas Fosterman's description of the situation. His confusion had quickly switched to intense anger. He no longer cared about the who and the why of the situation. The facts mattered little to him. He knew that this man had kidnapped him and was now threatening to kill him. All he cared about now was slaughtering this foolish old man.

He grabbed the rifle and placed it on the shooting mat. He threw on the earmuffs and grabbed the spotting scope setting it down at the top left corner of the mat. He laid down, sighted in and pulled the trigger. He had no idea where the shot had landed. It certainly didn't hit the panel, but he couldn't even see a dust cloud anywhere.

Rudy cursed at his himself. He knew better than to allow his temper to affect his shooting. He got up on his knees and squeezed his eyes shut. He unbuttoned his blue dress shirt and pulled it off using it as a rag to wipe the sweat from his brow. He untucked his white tank top and shook his arms trying to loosen the tension in his neck and shoulders. He cracked his neck to the left, then to the right before laying back down on the mat.

This time, Rudy took his time sighting in on the center black dot on the panel. He looked over at the range flag and saw that it was barely raised, measuring about five miles an hour of wind. He gave the scope three clicks to the left. He sighted back in on the target and tried to measure his breathing. He took a deep breath and exhaled. He gently squeezed the trigger firing his second round. There was a delay, then a loud thud.

Rudy grabbed the spotting scope and looked at the target. He could see that his shot had hit about two feet high and two feet to the left. He was just happy to hit the panel at this distance with his first solid try. He made a few more scope adjustments and sighted back in.

A Worthy Competitor

Lucas was still sitting in his chair waiting for Rudy's reaction when he heard the ring of the first shot. He saw a blast of sand fly into the air about 10 yards from the panel. He was somewhat relieved by the horrible shot. If this was how things were going to go, then Rudy didn't have a chance.

He waited three minutes before the second shot fired. This time it hit the panel. Lucas could see by the dent in the panel that it was only a couple of feet from the target. He felt a twinge of nerves, but quickly shook it off.

Ninety seconds later, a third shot rang out. This time the bullet was only 18 inches from the black.

A fourth shot; 12 inches from the black.

A fifth shot; 8 inches from the black. This time the shot was low and to the right. Rudy had overcompensated or pulled the trigger.

A sixth shot; back to 12 inches high and to the left.

A seventh shot, 4 inches from the black.

An eighth shot, this one caught the upper left-hand corner of the black silhouette.

A ninth shot, another hit, this time deeper into the black.

There was a delay before the tenth shot rang out.

At first, Lucas thought Rudy had missed, but then he noticed a dent on far left black target. He had switched targets. This shot was also in the black, about four inches away from the lower right-hand corner.

Lucas knew Rudy had to switch magazines at this point and wondered if he was done target practicing. About a minute later he heard the eleventh shot. He looked up to the far right black target and saw a dent just a couple of inches away from center mass.

Lucas was both impressed and terrified. He knew Rudy was an experienced shooter, but he was shocked that the man could sight in a rifle out to one mile in less than ten shots. Even more shocking was that he had put four shots in a row in the black. On Lucas' best days, he could only manage four in the black only after expending all twenty shots.

Looking down at his watch, we saw that it was 11:55. He picked up his cell phone and dialed the California Highway Patrol. He had a short conversation with a young lady dispatcher letting her know that someone had been killed at the GPS coordinates he had given her. She was still trying to get more details out of him when he cut the call short.

Lucas hadn't heard any shots in the past three minutes. He knew that Rudy was saving the rest of his ammunition.

Lucas grabbed a bottle of water from the cooler and took a few drinks. He wiped the sweat from his head, neck, shoulders and arms. Walking over to his shooting mat, he started his stretching routine. He followed the same series of twists, squats, and lunges that he always did before laying down on the mat.

He said a little prayer, asking God to give him strength and possibly some luck. Then he reached out and grabbed the rope attached to the 2x4 braces. He gave the rope a hard yank and the panel collapsed in a thud, leaving him exposed.

High Noon

After his eleventh target shot, Rudy Romero placed the rifle on safe and grabbed a bottle of water he had lying next to him. He drank it halfway down and recapped the bottle. Then he used his wadded up dress shirt to wipe his brow, arms, and hands.

He was more frustrated than angry at this point. He was frustrated about the heat, the sweating, the glare of the midday sun, the grating sand under his elbow. He was frustrated about the whole damn scenario.

He took a couple of minutes to recall all the white American men he knew and to go over the events of the past few days. He was searching for any clue as to who this Lucas Fosterman could be. He was certain that he did not know the man.

He was sure he had many enemies that he did not know. Could he be a hired assassin? Unlikely, given his age. A rival drug runner? Unlikely, given his age and race. Someone whose kid had been killed by his drugs? But how could anyone know whether or not they were his drugs, and how could they have found him?

That was the most frustrating part of all. How did someone know that he was going to be at that hotel, on that day, at that time, waiting for a car to take him to his appointment? That's when it hit him. The only person who knew his plans was Mariana. She must have betrayed him, but why? She lived like a queen, and she stood to lose everything. He couldn't believe Mariana would do this to him, but what other explanation could there be.

He was jarred back to attention by a thudding sound and a cloud of sand puffing up where the target panel had been. He quickly lined up behind the rifle, looked through the scope and switched off the safety. All he could see was a cloud of dust and sand.

Then he saw him. The old chauffeur was lying in a prone position mirror to his own. The old man was sighting in on his position, and he knew it wouldn't take long before the first shots rang out.

He was determined to be the first man to fire. He knew his biggest advantages were his age, steady hands, and sharp eyesight.

Quickly Now

Lucas was having a hell of a time trying to see through the dust cloud stirred up by the panel. He kept looking over the scope to make sure that he was lined up with the target. He knew he was wasting precious seconds, but there was nothing he could do to make the dust clear any faster. He settled back behind the rifle, moderately confident that he was pointed at the right angle.

He could see the outline of the white canopy come into focus. Then he started to see the shape of a man lying prone. He could tell that the barrel of the rifle was still moving left and right. He hadn't sighted in yet. Lucas settled in and prepared to take a shot. He took two deep breaths and exhaled slowly. He began to squeeze the trigger… *BLAM!*

Before he could get off a shot, he heard the crack of Rudy's rifle. A second later the wooden folding chair sitting behind him exploded into kindling. The sound of the rifle had caused Lucas to pull his trigger finger. His high-powered rifle fired at an odd angle, causing him to roll awkwardly to the left.

Lucas was now even more exposed, sitting up on his side with his rifle in the air. He was stunned by Rudy's speed and accuracy, but he had to get back into position. He shifted his weight to the right and started to roll back into position. Just as he started his roll a second crack rang out.

This time the bullet grazed the meaty part of his forearm. He winced at the searing pain, but continued his roll back into position. He glanced at the wound and saw that it was mostly superficial, but he could see a stream of blood and some meat showing. No time to deal with that now.

He quickly chambered a new round, sighted in, and fired. He knew that he probably wouldn't be on target for this one, but he had to start sending rounds down range.

Better Lucky than Good

Rudy was feeling good about himself at this point. He had seen the chair explode and was fairly sure that he had scored at least a glancing blow on the old man with his second shot. He was getting ready for a third shot when he heard the report of Lucas' rifle.

A foot-long hole appeared on the canopy ten feet above his head. He laughed at the man's horrible aim. But the shot had created a problem for him. The lucky projectile had created a hole just wide enough to allow the sun to shine directly into his scope. He would have to move over to get rid of the glare. To make matters worse, he now had a spotlight shining on him.

He shuffled hard to the right trying to stay as low as possible. He moved about six inches to the right, but he was still under the bright beam. As he made his second shuffle another shot fired. A blast of sand showered onto the right side of his body. He could feel small grains of sand fly into his face, arm, and shoulder. A searing pain coursed through his right eye. He squinted hard and pushed his face into his hands.

Blood started to appear in dots where the micro shrapnel had hit his arm and shoulder. But it was his eye that was the problem. Only one small piece of sand had pierced the corner of his right eye, but that was enough. The pain was excruciating. Worst of all, his right eye was his targeting eye.

Rudy buried his head in his hands and tucked in his shoulders trying to make himself as small of a target as possible. He squeezed his eyes shut as a stream of water and blood poured out of his right eye. He heard another shot fire and a bullet whiz by on his right, but there was no damage this time.

He tried to open his right eye, but it wouldn't budge. He could feel that it was swelling up, which made it more unlikely that he would be able to use it again anytime soon. He opened his left eye and focused on his hand. At least that eye was still working. It would have to do.

Another shot fired as he reached out to grab the rifle. Again, the shot went wide. He was sure it had passed on his right side again, but he wasn't sure how far off the shot had been. He lined the rifle back to its target and tried to focus his left eye on the scope. He felt uncomfortable in this position, but he had no choice but to return fire. He squeezed the trigger firing his thirteenth shot.

Quickly Man, Shoot

Lucas could tell that Rudy Romero had been injured by a shot that had landed just a couple of feet from the man and sprayed sand all over his right side. He had seen the man flinch and eventually lay flat with his head in his hands.

He took the opportunity to wrap his sweat rag around his bloody forearm. The makeshift tourniquet helped to stem the flow of blood, but it didn't stop it completely.

Lucas took advantage of the situation by firing off two quick shots. He jerked the trigger on the first shot, sending it way off target to the right. His shooting hand was attached to his injured arm and it was starting to go numb. He was even more unsteady on the second shot, sending it far to the right again.

His eyes widened when he saw that Rudy was getting back into position. He only had one more chance to hold his advantage. He closed his eyes for a second and took a deep breath. He opened his eyes, focused on his target, and took a second breath. Breathing out, he squeezed the trigger… Nothing happened.

Damn, he had forgotten to change magazines after his fifth shot. His nerves were failing him. For decades he had been shooting bolt-action rifles and the action of cycling the bolt should have been automatic muscle memory. Plus, he should have instinctively known that his magazine was empty.

Frustrated, he swapped out magazines, grabbed the bolt handle, ejected the old casing and chambered a new round. Rudy's thirteenth shot rang out. It passed overhead to his left, and he could tell that it was way off the mark.

Lucas looked through the scope and saw that Rudy was still lined up behind his rifle. He couldn't see what shape the man was in from this distance, but he couldn't be suffering too badly if he was already sending rounds down range again.

A fourteenth shot from Rudy, this time high and to the right.

Maybe his injuries were affecting his shooting.

Lucas tried to settle his trigger hand as he readied for another shot. He squeezed his bottom fingers hard around the bottom of the grip and gently pulled the trigger. The shot still missed to the right, even though he felt he had been fairly set this time.

That's when he noticed the range flag was now flying at 60 degrees, which meant that the wind had picked up to 15 miles-an-hour. He cursed himself for letting his discipline slip so badly over the past few minutes. This was no time for dumb mistakes. It was going to take a perfect shot to hit his mark, and he was far from perfect today.

Lucas heard Rudy's fifteenth shot fire, followed by a shower of black plastic pieces falling all around him. Rudy's bullet had hit the digital thermometer sitting on the table. It had been sitting about four feet directly over Lucas' head. He was getting close again.

On the Mark

After firing his fifteenth shot, Rudy was confident that he had properly adjusted his windage. Now he just needed to do an elevation change and make a good shot.

Rudy was surprised at how easy it had been to switch from his right eye to his left and remain accurate. He had learned long ago that military snipers shoot with both eyes open, and he had worked to develop the skill. He knew that the loss of his right eye would affect his depth perception to a degree, but it only took him three shots to make the adjustment.

His right eye had gone numb, but he could still feel a mix of blood and tears trickling down his chin and neck. The heat had caused the blood on the side of his face, arm, and hand to dry quickly and turn into a hard crust. He stretched out his neck and arm, before bearing down for another shot.

He heard another report from Lucas' side. Another miss, high and to the right. But getting closer. The previous three shots from the old man had been way off the mark. Rudy was sure that his adversary had not noticed the change in wind speed. Now, it looked like Lucas was getting dialed in.

Rudy took his time setting up for his sixteenth shot. He knew that his equipment was ready. Now he just needed to get in the proper frame of mind. He took a deep breath and squeezed his eyes shut. He opened his left eye and breathed out slowly.

Even the crack of another shot and the whizzing sound of a bullet flying just over his head didn't shake Rudy's resolve. He concentrated on his task.

As Lucas' form came into focus, he began squeezing the trigger. The rifles report startled him just a bit. He immediately knew he had made a good shot. After a one second delay, he could see the old man jerk to the left.

He had hit him!

A Bloody Mess

Lucas lay motionless on his left side. An intense burning pain coursed through the right side of his head. He was certain that his ear had been blown off along with his shattered earmuffs. The pressure from the bullet had instantly rocked him onto his side. His head was filled with a high-pitched ringing sound that overwhelmed his senses.

He could feel hot blood flowing from the side of his head and from his nose. He knew his time was short, and all he could think about was how he had let his family down. How he had let Hector down.

He had missed his chance to atone for his sins. He closed his eyes and tried to picture his wife Sarah and precious little Katie. But they weren't there. The only image he could see was the sight of Jim Powers dying from the gunshot wound to his stomach. It was the image that had haunted him every day since he had murdered the man.

He had believed that righteousness was on his side. That should have been enough. Now he was going to die here in the desert without completing his mission. He hadn't made things better. He had made things much worse.

He had been so close. His last shot had been centered on the target. It was just a bit high. He only needed one more shot, and he would have atoned for his past and made things right again.

The ringing sound in Lucas' head started to subside a bit, but the blood continued to flow. He tried to move his right arm and felt that he was still holding the rifle. He could feel that his left arm was also still gripping the rifle.

He tried to think through his last actions. He had fired a shot. It was a good shot. He had ejected the cartridge and slid the bolt home. Then bam.

That was it. His rifle was ready. It was ready to fire.

He knew that he didn't have much time. The blood was flowing freely from his head, nose, and forearm. He didn't know if he could even sight in on a target and pull the trigger. Hell, he didn't even know if he could get back into position before Rudy finished him off. But he had to try.

Lucas tensed every muscle he had and moved to roll back into his shooting position. He let out a loud yell as his body slammed down on the shooting mat.

Oh, Hell

Rudy Romero was looking through the spotting scope trying to confirm that the old man was indeed dead. He knew the shot had been a solid one, and he had even seen a splash of red in his scope. When Lucas' body had flopped to the side, he had gritted his teeth and hissed in excitement.

Through the lens of the spotting scope, he could see that the old man was indeed lying on his side with blood covering the side of his head. He watched for any signs of life, but couldn't see any. He was too far away to tell if the man was still breathing or not, but he should be able to see movement.

He chuckled to himself as he thought about how foolish this Lucas Fosterman had been to think that he could defeat him. He had been at the range at least three days a week for the past twenty years. He was as good a marksman as any military or police sniper. Plus, he had killed dozens of men in his life. It really had been a foolish attempt.

He was getting ready to put down the spotting scope, when he saw the body of the old man flop down with the rifle still in his hands. He stared out in shock for a second before throwing the scope to the side and grabbing his rifle. He looked through the scope and saw that Lucas was already in shooting position.

He placed his hand on the grip and moved his finger onto the trigger. He took a deep breath and focused in on the target. Then he heard the crack of a rifle.

Mission Accomplished

Lucas watched as a cloud of pink appeared in his scope.

It had taken all he had to bear down and make one last good shot. He had been forced to release the tourniquet around his forearm in order to regain movement in his trigger hand.

He knew he only had one shot, so he made sure it was the best shot he could make given his condition. He had aimed about two feet low, and it had been right on the mark given the amount of pink spray he had seen.

His right arm slumped to the side. Lucas released his grip on the rifle and allowed his body to roll back to his left. He couldn't stop his momentum and ended up crashing down on his back.

He was now facing up at the white canopy. He could see the shadows of large white clouds slowly crawling their way across the sky.

The ringing in his head had dulled to a dim hum by this point. He could still feel the blood flowing from his body, but the pain was nearly gone. He felt a sense of accomplishment, knowing that he had completed his mission. He had atoned for his sins.

He closed his eyes waiting for the image of Sarah and his precious little Katie to fill his mind.

There was nothing at first, then it came. The image of Jim Powers' dead eyes, this time followed by a pink cloud exploding from the back of Rudy Romero's head.

Tears started to flow from Lucas' eyes as he knew this would be the last image he ever saw.

Epilogue

"In this sad world of ours, sorrow comes to all; and, to the young, it comes with bitterest agony, because it takes them anawares."

— Abraham Lincoln

The Bloody Desert

California Highway Patrol Officer Jennifer Danver was making her way through the desert backroads trying to find her way to the coordinates the dispatcher had given her.

She had received the confusing call about an hour ago. She had just finished a traffic stop near Felicity and had to fill up with gas and water before heading so far out into the desert.

She knew there was a high probability that the call was a false alarm or some sort of prank, but the dispatcher said she thought the man who made the call had sounded sincere. She hated traveling this far into the desert through mostly uncharted backroads without any prior notice or backup nearby. At least it was early afternoon, and she had plenty of time to get back before dark, that is if the call really was a false alarm.

After two hours of driving and several wrong turns, she could see on her GPS that she was getting close to the coordinates. She crested a small area of dunes and could now see for miles in front of her. What looked to be a white canopy was sitting straight ahead along with a black sedan. *I guess this might*

193

not be a false alarm after all.

As she pulled up next to a black Lincoln Town Car parked next to the white canopy she could see that a second canopy was sitting far off into the distance. The scene was definitely odd. She could see an old man lying at the front of the canopy. He was covered in blood and appeared to be dead.

She got out of the car and pulled her service revolver. First, she inspected the Town Car. She threw open the door and looked inside, nothing. She also popped the trunk and went around back for a closer inspection. She kicked the trunk lid open with her foot and looked inside, nothing.

She looked around in every direction, but realized there was nowhere else to hide. She walked over to the old man, keeping her revolver out and checked his pulse. He was dead.

She holstered her pistol and grabbed a pair of binoculars lying in the sand a few feet away from the body. She brushed them off and looked through the lens at the other white canopy. She could see that the scene was a near mirror image. She noticed another body, lying on its back and covered in blood. There was no need to check for a pulse on that body. She could see that the man's head had been blown half off. She scanned the area for any other signs of life. Finding none, she decided it was time to call it in.

"Dispatch, this is Officer Danver."

"Go ahead."

"Dispatch, I'm at the coordinates that were provided. We have two fatalities and two apparent murder scenes. We are going to need forensic teams on site and a detective."

The Call

Mark Fosterman was sitting in his kitchen drinking coffee when he heard the phone ring. Who would be calling this early in the morning?

"Mister Fosterman?" A feminine voice inquired.

"Yes."

"Mark Fosterman, son of Lucas Fosterman."

"Yes," Mark was becoming confused. "How can I help you?"

"My name is Officer Jennifer Danver with the California Highway Patrol, and I have some news about your father."

"My father? Are you sure? My dad is in Missouri." Mark was starting to feel uneasy. He hadn't heard from his dad all weekend, which wasn't usual. He just figured he had been caught up telling war stories with his old buddies in Branson.

"I'm sorry to tell you that your father is definitely in California. I'm also sorry to tell you that he died last night."

"I don't understand. He has been sick, but he seemed fine just a few days ago. He is supposed to be in Southern Missouri visiting with friends."

"Was your father driving a 1966 Chevy Pickup registered in your name?"

"Yes."

"I'm not sure what to say Mister Fosterman, but I'm certain that we found your father's body last night in the desert east of Yuma."

Mark was stunned and confused. It just didn't make any sense. He racked his brain trying to figure out what it all meant. He was drawing a complete blank.

"Mister Fosterman… Mister Fosterman… Are you still there?"

"Yes, yes… Sorry, I am just having a problem processing all of this."

"Mister Fosterman, do you know a man named Rudy Romero?"

After another ten minutes of confusing conversation, Mark hung up the phone. He sat at the table rubbing his head. He was still trying to process all the information the officer had told him.

His father was dead. He was in California. He had died due to loss of blood from multiple rifle wounds. His truck was found at the Hotel Del Coronado. He had shot a man named Rudy

Romero in the head. This Romero guy ran some sort of drug cartel. His dad's body would need to stay at the morgue until an autopsy could be performed. He needed to arrange for the truck to be picked up from the evidence impound lot in about a week.

Just then, Lisa walked down the stairs still wearing her night gown. She headed straight for the coffee. "Who was that calling so early this morning? It wasn't your dad was it? For an old man, he gets up earlier than anyone I know."

Not getting a response, she looked over at Mark. He was now starting to cry. It would take him a long time to understand everything that he had heard this morning, but the one thing he did understand was that his dad was dead.

"Oh God, Mark. What's wrong?"

It took Mark a while to explain everything to Lisa, who had more questions than he had answers. They spent the next hour conducting a mini investigation. They called Lucas' friends in Branson who knew nothing about a planned visit. They called the Hotel Del Coronado who said that Lucas has made the reservation three weeks ago. They researched the internet and found out that Rudy Romero was the head of a Colombian drug cartel. News of his death was just starting to hit the networks, but there still wasn't any mention of Lucas... thank God.

Mark decided it was time to call his brother Paul and the rest of the family. He didn't want them to hear about Dad's death on the news.

FedEx Arrives

It was 4 pm and Mark's kitchen and living room were filled with family members and friends. Everyone had been shocked at the news, and no one had any answers. Most of them were in the living room watching the news on TV, as Paul surfed from one news channel to the next waiting for the latest updates.

The news had started showing Lucas' name and his mug shot

at around noon, which caused a flurry of phone calls. Everyone was a bit startled to see Lucas depicted as a common criminal. From an outsider's perspective it probably looked like Lucas had been hired in prison to make a hit on the cartel leader, but those who knew Lucas knew that wasn't possible.

Still, no one had any theories as to how this had happened.

Federal agents from the FBI had stopped by earlier in the day to question various people in the house. None of them had much to offer. After a couple hours of questions, even the federal agents didn't seem to understand what had happened.

At around 5 pm everyone started to leave. Now only Mark, Lisa, and Paul were left sitting around the table. They sat in numb silence for a while, until a ring from the doorbell caused Mark to jump. He opened the door and was handed a FedEx envelope from the uniformed deliveryman.

He looked over the address label and saw that it was addressed to him. The from address just showed Hotel Del Coronado. He felt the hair stand up on the back of his neck.

He opened the envelope and pulled out a set of his dad's truck keys. He then pulled out a letter that had his and Paul's name written on the front in his father's handwriting. He opened the letter feeling a sense of déjà vu and began reading.

Dear Mark and Paul,

Once you get this letter, I will likely be dead. I'm sure someone has informed you by now. You are probably confused as to how your father ended up dead in a desert in California.

I wish I had a good answer for you. I can only say that I am hoping to find a way to atone for my transgressions.

At first I felt justified in killing the man that took away our precious little Katie. I was comforted when I saw how it allowed everyone in the family to start moving on with their lives. I was heartened by the many letters and visitors who told me how proud they were of me for taking action against that evil man. But deep down, I knew that none of that mattered. It didn't matter because I knew the truth. I didn't really kill that man for justice. I didn't really kill him for the family. I didn't even kill him for Katie. I killed him out of hate...

Epilogue

I killed him for myself. I wanted him dead. I needed him to be dead.

For the past ten years, the image of him dying and the light fading from his eyes has haunted me every day. I have prayed every day for forgiveness. Maybe God has forgiven me, I really don't know. But I know I haven't forgiven myself.

I worked hard to be helpful to other people in prison. I taught them skills, helped them earn degrees, counselled them about addiction, and prayed for them daily. I did everything I could to make amends.

It wasn't until I met a young man named Hector Morales and found out that I was being sent home that I knew I might have a real chance at redemption. This young man has lived a life in captivity, surrounded by fear and pain. I believe I have a chance to release him and his family from that captivity and from that pain, so that is what I am planning to do.

I don't know if I will accomplish my mission, but either way, I don't believe I will be coming home. The doctors say I will be lucky to make it another few weeks, and my mission will likely push me beyond my physical limits.

Take care of the family. Try to remember the good times we had together and erase the foolishness I have caused of over the past ten years from memory. They have been the actions of a sad old man trying to find atonement. Find a way to join his dearest Sarah and Katie in heaven.

I hope to see her there. I hope to see you all there someday.

Your Loving Father

About the Author

Jason Mayer spent the first part of his adult life as a Marine Corps Combat Correspondent covering stories on five continents and more than 50 countries. After leaving the Marine Corps, he spent eight years working with a government contractor supervising the development of more than 200 annual publishing projects. Today, Jason is an owner and partner in a number of companies including a construction company that designs, sells, and manages specialty construction projects and a publishing company that specializes in community newcomer and business guides. He has degrees in Communications and Business Management and an MBA from the University of Maryland. Jason lives in Columbia, Missouri with his wife Angela and two boys, Noah and Caleb.